RUDIE DUDIE

The Jiggy McCue books can be read in any order, but to get the most out of them (Jiggy and Co are a wee bit older in each one) we suggest you read them in the following order:

Visit Michael Lawrence's website:
www.wordybug.com

And find loads of Jiggy fun at:
www.jiggymccue.com

A JIGGY McCUE STORY

RUDIE DUDIE

MICHAEL LAWRENCE

ORCHARD BOOKS

ORCHARD BOOKS
338 Euston Road, London NW1 3BH
Orchard Books Australia
Level 17/207 Kent Street, Sydney, NSW 2000

First published in 2010 by Orchard Books

ISBN 978 1 40830 483 9

Text © Michael Lawrence 2010
Illustrations © Steve May 2010

The rights of Michael Lawrence to be identified as the author and Steve
May to be identified as the illustrator of this work have been asserted by them
in accordance with the Copyright, Designs and Patents Act, 1988.

A CIP catalogue record for this book is available from the British Library.

3 5 7 9 10 8 6 4 2

Printed in Great Britain

Orchard Books is a division of Hachette Children's Books,
an Hachette UK company.

www.hachette.co.uk

To Brother Martin,
golfer, walker, quatmeister,
discoverer of flailing family lines

CHAPTER ONE

Teachers should be banned. Some of them at least. The ones who shout all the time for no reason. The ones whose middle name is Detention. The ones who put a hex on you that makes you drop your pants and flash your bum in public places. Yes, I know the last of these is a bit unusual. In your life anyway. But you're not Jiggy McCue. Jiggyworld seems to be ruled by nutters like that.

The teacher who made me flash my basement cheeks was new at Ranting Lane. Her name Ms Mooney. Our first sight of her was on day one of the new school year, when all the classes were jammed into the main hall to be welcomed, warned about misbehaving and introduced to her from the stage. She was unlike any teacher we ever saw. She had this tragic fright-wig type hair (orange) and a nose that flipped up at the end, and she wore very jazzy clothes that didn't match anything in sight, and all these bangles that rattled, and a clunky necklace that looked like bits of coloured rock. She was also shorter than every boy over twelve except Eejit Atkins, though we didn't realise it till our first lesson with her. This occurred the first Wednesday afternoon of term, in the gym. Her lessons were to take place there because we would need space for them, apparently. Ms Mooney was taking us for Drama. Drama. Like I needed more of it in my life.

We soon learnt when we met her nose to turned-up nose that this teacher wasn't one you could relax with. She had this quick, jerky way of moving, and she hardly ever smiled. But the most unrelaxing thing about her was her eyes. They were like twin black holes. There was something familiar about those eyes – and her expression when she stared – but if I'd seen her before I couldn't remember where.

The first thing Ms Mooney got us to do when she came into the gym for Drama lesson one was tell her our names. Naturally, we tried the all-at-once routine, but she shouted us down and told us to start again, one at a time, alphabetical order. There was a bit of a hiccup here because Atkins is the second name in the register and he's not so hot at the alphabet. After him the name-giving went OK until I said mine and Miss stopped Angie Mint, who's next, and asked me to say it again. I was tempted to say 'Vladimir Putin' this time, but I played it straight because she was new. When she didn't seem to catch my name the second time either, though, I said:

'Hey, Miss, if the old lugs are blocked I could bring in a bog plunger from home.'

This touch of good cheer was out half a split second before I noticed that she had bigger ears than normal. Her huge dangly earrings didn't do them any favours – in fact they drew your attention to them, but unfortunately they hadn't drawn mine soon enough. There were a few giggles and chuckles, but none from Ms Mooney.

'What sort of name's Jiggy?' she asked coldly.

I frowned. Ears or no ears, no one casts nasturtiums on my name, even teachers. 'What sort of name's Mooney?' I zapped back.

She narrowed her eyes, and a blast of cold air whistled through my bones. But I tried not to show that she made me nervous. Show nervousness to a new teacher and they immediately think they

9

have you where they want you instead of the other way round.

'You find my name amusing?' she said.

'Amusing?' I replied. 'No. Makes me think of mooning, that's all.'

'Mooning?'

'Dropping your nicks and dazzling strangers with your rear end.'

'I see.' She paused. Then she said: 'Jiggy, eh? I'll remember that.'

And she turned away, slowly and sort of deliberately, like she'd just made a threat. Our relationship had not got off to a perfect start.

When she'd got all our names, Ms Mooney told us what we were going to do in her lesson. A Shakespeare play. There were groans from at least half the class. One of the ones who didn't groan was Julia Frame.

'Brilliant!' she said, clapping her stupid hands. 'I love Shakespeare!'

But instead of turning a beam of teacherly delight on her, Miss flashed the black-hole orbs and said, in a voice straight out of the freezer: '*Do you now?*'

Julia didn't pick up on the ice, maybe because she was so thrilled about doing Willy-boy. 'Oo, yes, Miss. I know all his plays. Well, most of them. My dad's mad about them. He used to read them to me at bedtime!'

'Before they carted him off to the whack-house,' muttered Ryan.

'Quiet!' Ms M said. 'All of you!'

When most teachers say something like that it's about twenty minutes before we let silence take over, but there was something about this one that you didn't argue with. There was an instant hush.

'The play, in which *some* of you will perform –' (a glare at Julia) '– is *A Midsummer Night's Dream*. But we'll be under—'

'Oo, my favourite!' Julia said excitedly.

'—under some pressure thanks to the time of year. We have a lot to get through by the half-term break, before which we'll perform it in front of other pupils, parents and teachers.'

'Perform it?' someone squawked.

'In public?' squawked someone else.

'But half term's only weeks away!' squawked a third.

'Indeed. And as our lesson occupies a mere hour once a week those taking part will be working all the free hours their homework will permit.'

'Why have we got to do it in such a rush, Miss?' Angie asked.

'Because I have a very different play to organise with another class in the run-up to Christmas,' Miss explained. She didn't sound pleased about this.

'What play's that then?' Majid Aziz piped up, like he cared.

Ms Mooney glared at the ground rather than him. 'A script has yet to be written, but I'm informed that it's to be a multicultural nonpartisan drama that takes care not to offend any minority religious faction or politically correct sensibility. In other words, a Christmas play that has nothing *whatsoever* to do with Christmas!'

'Can we get started on ours, Miss?' Julia asked eagerly. The half of the class that had groaned when they first heard about it turned to her and hissed. She shrank back. 'Well, we haven't got much time to work on it,' she said. 'And *A Midsummer Night's Dream*'s quite long.'

'I've cut it to about forty minutes,' Ms Mooney said.

Julia gasped. 'Forty minutes? You can't cut *A Midsummer Night's Dream* to forty minutes!'

'Well, I *have*!' Miss snapped. 'Now be quiet while I tell the rest of the class what the play's about.'

'Some of us know already,' Kelly Ironmonger said. 'I saw the film with Kevin Kline.'

'Bet you had to bribe him,' said Wapshott.

'In *essence*,' Miss went on frostily, '*A Midsummer Night's Dream* is a light-hearted entertainment about the nature of love.' (Forehead slaps from all the boys except Martin Skinner.) 'In the original, the main events take place in the forest home of the fairies, where—'

'Fairies!' several boys cried in horror.

'—where the lives of four sweethearts fall apart due to mix-ups and the intervention of Oberon, the fairy king.'

'I'm not playing no king fairy,' one of us muttered.

'Being a Shakespeare comedy there is, naturally, a fair amount of mischief, much of which is provided by an impish fairy called Puck –' (muffled chortles) '– who at Oberon's behest brews a magic love juice to put on the eyelids of his queen, Titania –' (more chortles) '– as a punishment for disobeying him.

Oberon's idea is that the love juice will make Titania fall hopelessly for the first lowly creature she sees when she wakes. Unfortunately, the first creature she claps eyes on is Nick Bottom the weaver.'

Howls of laughter at this. Miss turned on one of the howlers like he was the only one doubled up with hysterics.

'I imagine that it's the name *Bottom* that so entertains my new friend Jiggy McKee?'

I killed the hysteria. 'McCue, Miss. McCue. OK? And I wasn't the only one laughing.'

'Your laughs were louder than the others.'

'Yeah, well, I have this tonsil condition.'

'There's much more to the plot, of course,' Ms M said, turning away, 'but we'll come to it as we come to it. As I've had to cut the play to a serviceable length I've adapted the story to fit the forest scenes. That way we don't have to change the scenery. And instead of a forest, I thought, to make things easier still, we would set it in a modern classroom.'

This wasn't well received. We see enough classrooms every day without setting a play in one.

'You'd rather the action took place in a forest?' Miss asked.

'Yeah, one far, far away,' said Ryan.

'If we set it in a forest, we'll have to make substantial scenery and a number of props, to say nothing of costumes. That would mean a lot of work for some of you. Are you sure you want to do all that when we could simply use a few desks and the actors could wear their existing school uniforms?'

While most of us went suddenly dumb (as in silent) a few nutters said 'Yay' and the yays must have done it for Ms Mooney, because suddenly it was a sealed deal. There would be a forest, props and costumes, all made by us, like we had nothing better to do with our lives.

'What we have to do now,' Miss said next, 'is choose our actors. Some of you will be keen to be in the play, I know, and some won't, so let's start by finding out which is which. Those of you who would really like to be in *A Midsummer Night's Dream* go and stand on that side of the room.'

About a third of the class (all girls except Skinner) immediately headed that way, smiling happily, like they'd just achieved a lifetime's ambition.

'You want to be in it?' I said in amazement as Angie passed me.

'Yeah, why not? Chance to show my star quality. Hope I get queen of the fairies.'

'Titty,' said Pete.

'Titania!' said Julia Frame sharply. No surprise that she was with the mob that wanted to be in the thing.

'Now just to be certain that we know who wants to do it and who doesn't,' Ms Mooney said, 'all of you who wouldn't touch a Shakespeare play with a bargepole please go and stand on the other side.'

Almost all of the rest of us, including some girls and Marlene Bronson, veered sharply to the right wearing relieved smirks. We'd got out of it! And so easily!

The only one left standing in the middle was Eejit Atkins.

'Ralph?' Ms M said to him. 'Which group are you with?'

'I dunno,' he answered. 'I din't unnerstan' the queschun.'

She left him where he was and told those of us who didn't want to be in the play to call our names out. She wrote them in a little notebook, then said (to us, not the other lot): 'I don't know if we can find parts for all of you – might have to have more fairies than the script demands – but we'll see how it goes.'

Everyone in our group looked at everyone else in our group, puzzled. We were still doing this when Miss came over to us.

'Now who shall play who, I wonder…'

Time to speak up. 'No, Miss, you've got it wrong,' I said. 'We're the ones who wouldn't touch this thing with a midsummer bargepole. The ones you want are over there. Skinner would make a great fairy king.'

She turned her black eyes on me. 'No, *you've* got it wrong…Jiggy. My purpose here is to involve those who think they would *not* like to be in a play. It's from *your* group that my actors will be chosen!'

Any lingering smirks of relief hit the floor with the most dramatic kerplunk in drama history.

CHAPTER TWO

'I changed my mind,' said Ryan. 'I want to act.' He started across the room to join Skinner and the girls.

'I'm glad to hear it,' Ms Mooney said. 'You can be Peaseblossom.'

Ryan's heels ground twin grooves in the parquet flooring.

'What!'

'Peaseblossom,' Miss repeated. 'One of Titania's faithful fairies.'

Steam shot out of Ryan's ears. Ryan sees himself as Mr Macho. Does a lot of shoulder-rolling and knees-out swaggering and thumping other boys when teachers aren't looking.

'I'm not playing a bleeding fairy.'

'Oh, but you are,' said Miss.

'No way. Not me.'

She went to him. Looked up at him.

'Bryan, isn't it?' she said.

'Yeah…?'

'Well, Bryan. You are now officially Fairy Peaseblossom. Let's *not* have any argument about that, mm?'

There was a pause while Ryan scowled down at her. And then…his expression changed, his features softened, like he'd just been offered an autograph by a top footie star with a thick wife.

'OK, Miss.'

A gasp from quite a few of us. There was this little woman in these mad clothes, with this insane orange hair and swinging earrings, looking up at him, and he, Ryan, who worked out all the time because he wanted a corrugated stomach, had folded, just like that.

'Now go and sit on the floor by the exercise mats please,' Miss said.

And Ryan went, meek as a mitten, and sat down, legs crossed, looking at his hands like he was wondering why they hadn't picked her up and hung her from the ceiling by her batty hair. This was worrying. If she could make Ryan play a fairy without a fight…

'Miss, can I be in it please? I really want to be

in it, and I know the play!'

Julia Frame, with the other team. She looked keen. Wide-eyed keen. Ms M frowned.

'I've explained my decision, Julia.'

'I know, but—'

'I have *explained* it.' Julia closed her mouth. 'But never fear, everyone will contribute something to the production.'

'Miss?' Angie had raised her hand.

'Yes... Angela, is it?'

'Angie. What if I said I didn't want to act after all?'

'Then I would say fine, you can paint scenery.'

'But I'm lousy at painting.'

'Well here's your chance to improve. Apply yourself and you might discover hidden talents. Wouldn't that be nice?'

'No,' said Ange, turning her bottom lip into a dinner plate.

While all this was going on, Pete and I were trying to get to the back of our group so we wouldn't be picked for anything major. The trouble with that was that everyone else was trying to get to the back too, so in the end what you got was a big bunch of kids *all* at the back, trying to put everyone else in front.

Ms Mooney turned to us. 'Let's see now. Who among you will play the main parts?'

'Him! Him! Him! Her!' shouted half a dozen voices at once. Mine and Pete's voices weren't among them. We'd ducked down behind the rest and were keeping shtum.

'You two,' said Ms Mooney.

Our group fell silent as everyone avoided her sharp black eyes, hoping she didn't mean them.

'The two crouching down at the back.'

Our group parted in the middle to reveal Pete and me, squatting.

'Yes, you. You seem to be especially keen not to be chosen. Here please.'

We eyed the door, trying to estimate our chances of getting through it before our collars were grabbed.

'Stop dallying,' said Miss. 'Here. Now.'

We stood up and mooched forward.

'I have a policy,' Ms M said when we were standing in front of her.

'Hey, so's my dad,' I said, trying to lighten

21

things up a bit. 'Fully comprehensive, including storm and flood damage. What's yours for?'

'My policy,' she said, like I hadn't spoken, 'is to introduce the least keen to great dramatic works in the hope that they'll grow to love them. The best way to do that, I've found, is to give those reluctant souls some prominence. You'd be surprised how many find that they enjoy speaking language that's not of the streets once they get used to it.'

Pete and I traded glances. What was the ancient loon *on* about?

'What I'm *on* about,' she said (we jumped; was she *psychic* or something?), 'is that your unwillingness to participate has led to your being given starring roles.'

'What?' I said.

'What?' said Pete.

'Now who shall you be?' She folded her arms under her bosoms, which made them stare at us like a pair of extra eyes. 'I'm a firm believer in casting against type, so…yeees…'

She was looking Pete up and down.

'What?' he said again, nervously this time.

'Oberon. You will play Oberon.'

'Who?'

'I see him as tall, powerful, charismatic, everything you're not. Congratulations, the part's yours.'

'Obe-Wan?' Pete said. 'Does he have a lightsaber?'

'Obe-*ron*, and no, he doesn't. Though as king of the fairies I suppose you could carry a wand of some sort if it pleases you.'

'King of the f…?' said Pete. 'King of the f…? You want me to play the king of the f…?'

He couldn't bring himself to say it, and I don't blame him.

'I do, yes. And you will, so don't bother to argue.'

While their conversation was going on I'd started to edge sideways, hoping that if I edged far enough she'd forget I existed and pick on someone else. It's quite cosy in my dream world.

'Now. *Jiggy*.'

She said my name like it was something that had given her heartburn. I stopped the sideways edge.

'The part I have in mind for you isn't that far against type,' Ms Mooney said to me. 'In fact, from what's been said so far in our brief acquaintance, I'm guessing that it will fit you to a T.'

'I don't like tea much,' I said.

'You are going to play…' She waited, so I could get the full dramatic impact of the word that followed: 'Bottom.'

Some members of the class giggled. I wasn't one of them.

'Hey, now wait a minute,' I said.

'No need,' she said. 'You're going to be Bottom. Nick Bottom is a cocky character who likes to be the focus of attention. When the amateur dramatics troop of which he's a member decides to put on a play – a play within a play, you see – he thinks he can play all the parts himself.'

'I don't want to play all the parts,' I said. 'I don't want *any* part.'

'Which is precisely why you have one,' said Miss. 'And such an important one at that. To give you a chance to really get into the role, I'd better tell you of a certain key incident in the play.'

'Key incident?'

'When the mischievous Puck spots the actors rehearsing in the forest, he turns Bottom's head into…?' She glanced at Julia Frame.

'An ass's,' Julia said sulkily.

Ms Mooney smiled at me for the first time. Not a very nice smile.

'An ass's. Bottom spends a good portion of the play as an ass. As I say, excellent casting.'

More giggles from the class. Still not from me.

'Have I got to wear wings, Miss?' Pete said.

She turned to him. 'Wings?'

'If I'm King Fairy.'

'No, no. Oberon isn't that kind of fairy.' She turned away. 'Ralph. Here please, I have a part for you too.'

Eejit came over. 'Ya do?'

'I do. You will play Puck.'

'Puck? 'Owja spell it?'

'As it sounds. Puck is the one who turns Bottom here into an ass.'

'Cor,' said Eejit, glancing at my backside.

I scowled. 'Turn me into an ass, Atkins, and you're porridge.'

Eejit was all teeth. Suddenly he saw his manky name in lights.

'Now let's see who we can cast for the other parts…' Miss said.

CHAPTER THREE

By hometime all the parts had been assigned and Ms Mooney had handed out copies of the script for us to study before next week's lesson. There was a lot of unhappy grumbling as we shuffled through the gates that afternoon. We Chosen Ones were grumbling because we didn't want to be in a school play and the kids from the other group were grumbling because they did, and weren't. Dob Hegarty was moaning about never living down the part he'd been stuck with. Hegarty's one of the tallest kids in the class, and he has a nose like a beak, and lots of dark curly hair, and he likes fighting, and Mooney had given him a part that brought even more laughs than mine.

'Titania?' Hegarty gasped when she told him. 'But isn't that a…female?'

'I certainly hope so,' Miss replied. 'She's the queen of the fairies.'

'Queen of the f… queen of the f…' It was Pete all

over again, but worse somehow. At least Pete was playing a *male* fairy.

'But it's appropriate for a boy to play her,' Ms Mooney added. 'In Shakespeare's day, female parts were played by boys or young men. Females weren't allowed to act on the stage.'

'Sexism goes way back then,' Laura Porritt said.

'It does indeed.'

'Miss, this isn't Shakespeare's day,' said Hegarty.

'Well, let's pretend it is, shall we? You're Titania. Live with it.'

She turned away, and all Hegarty could do was stare at Pete, who was staring at him. They were married!

Angie was another one who wasn't in the greatest of moods as we headed homeward. She'd wanted Hegarty's part, and she hadn't got it. Or any other.

'I've never been in a school play,' she said to her chest.

'You have,' I said.

She looked up. 'When?'

'Infants. Nativity play.'

'That was years ago.'

27

'It was still a play. You were one of the three bearded wise men in dressing gowns. I was another. Pete was an angel with a wonky halo made of pipe cleaners and tinsel.'

'You were the wise man who brought the gold,' Angie said. 'How jammy can you get? All I had was myrrh. Myrrh! I don't even know what it is and I'm giving it to this brat as a birthday gift!'

'Sap,' said Pete.

She whirled on him. 'What did you call me?'

'Not you. Myrrh. It's dried tree sap.'

'How the hell do you know that?'

'I read it in the downstairs loo.'

'What downstairs loo?'

'Ours. At home. *The Little Book of Stuff You Really Don't Need to Know* that my dad put there to help pass the time.'

'Why would anyone give a baby dried tree sap?' Angie demanded, like it was his idea.

'No Toys R Us in those days,' Pete said.

'I'd have binned the myrrh along with the frankincense if I'd been the birthday boy,' I said. 'Specially if the chocolate coins had been real gold. If they'd been real, I'd have crawled away with them while my parents were still laying why-thank-you-so-much smirks on the hairy whackos who thought they'd brought such cool gifts. Did she look familiar?'

'Who?' said Angie.

'Mooney.'

'Not to me.'

'Pete?'

'No. Why?'

'I'm sure I've seen her before.'

'Where?'

'Can't remember.'

'When?'

'Dunno.'

'Which means you probably haven't,' Angie said.

'No, I have, I know I have…'

When we reached our street, they headed for their house and I headed for mine. That's the cunning way we do things on the Brook Farm Estate. I didn't tell Mum and Dad about the play. Didn't need to as it happened, because Angie's ma phoned mine later to spread the news. Mum couldn't have been more amazed if I'd suddenly turned into a goldfish.

'You've been cast in *A Midsummer Night's Dream*!' she said. 'You! My son! In a play!'

Her eyes were like SOS flares. I knew why. She was seeing me as a chip off the old mother block.*

'Wasn't my idea,' I said. 'I was railroaded by this new teacher from the asylum.'

'You didn't volunteer then?'

'Volunteer to play someone called Bottom? Oh sure, just up my alley, that.'

'Bottom's a great comic part,' she said.

'Yeah, right, I won't able to sleep tonight for laughing.'

She hugged me to her bosom. 'Well, I'm very proud of you.'

I pushed her away. 'Don't be. I'm gonna be rubbish.'

'No you're not.'

'Trust me, I am.'

When Dad came in she told him. He wasn't so impressed.

'I hated Shakespeare at school,' he said.

'Oh, in your class, was he?' said I.

'We had to read him, in English, week after week, out loud. Didn't do any of his lousy plays,

---

* She'd recently joined this local amateur dramatics group and never stopped talking about it.

though, I'm glad to say.'

'Lucky you.'

'But I was in another school play.'

'Yeah, what was that?'

'*Toad of Toad Hall*. I had one of the main parts actually.'

'You didn't play Toad!' Mum said in amazement.

'No, I was Ratty.'

She got unamazed. 'What, even as a boy?'

I was bringing Swoozie up to speed on the whole play deal when Pete and Angie came over. Swoozie's my baby sister. She's too young to have a really intelligent conversation with, but the way she looks at me when I talk to her, I know she's doing her best to keep up.

'Angie and Pete for you, Jig!' Mum yelled up the stairs.

'I'm talking to Suzie!' I yelled down. (I have to call her Suzie when speaking to Mum and Dad because they don't know that she's going to call herself Swoozie one day.)*

'She should be asleep!' Mum yelled back.

'She was till you started yelling!'

---

* To find out how Jiggy knows, see *The Iron, the Switch and the Broom Cupboard*.

'Well, leave her! Angie and Pete are here!'

'So you said! I'm coming!' I leant over my little sister's little cot. 'See ya later, Swooze,' I said.

She gummed up at me, rosy-cheeked, bubble-mouthed. This meant, 'See ya later, Jig.'

Mum had left Pete and Angie in the hall, where Ange was thumping Pete while he tried to fend her off with his copy of Ms Mooney's script.

'I'm sorry, all right?' he said. 'How many more times?'

'What's he done now?' I asked, galloping down.

'What's he done now?' Angie replied. 'What's he done *now*?'

'Yeah, what's he done now?'

'Ask *him*!' she said, still thumping.

'What have you done, Garrett?'

'I'll tell you what he's done!' said Ange. 'He microwaved a fly!'

'He what?'

'Turned the microwave on with a fly inside!'

'Flies deserve everything they get,' said Pete.

'You mean he did it accidentally?' I said.

'No, I do not mean he did it –' *thump, thump* '– accidentally. I mean the little weasel saw the fly fly

32

in, slammed the door –' *thump* '– and turned the thing on. Deliberately!'

'I wanted to see what'd happen,' Pete said, cowering.

'It was a living *creature*!' she said.

'Living creatures die all the time.'

'NOT IN MICROWAVES, YOU SOILED BOG BRUSH!'

'Well, I won't do it again, that's a promise, OK?'

'You'd better not!'

'No need to. I know what happens now.'

We went up to my room. There I asked Pete why he'd brought his script.

'We're supposed to study it,' he said.

I snatched it off him, frowned at the front page and shoved it back into his hands.

'Consider it studied. Now what shall we do?'

'I've never seen a play script before,' he said, flipping through it like it was the fourteenth wonder of the world.

'Well now you have, so put it away.'

'I never played a *king* before either.'

'Garrett, there's kings and there's *fairy* kings. You're one of the fairy kind.'

'Still,' he said. 'A king. Step up from a school kid.'

'Only if you don't think royals are a waste of flesh, blood and bone,' I said.

'You're starting to sound like your dad,' Angie said.

'That's because both our voices have broken. Pete. Look. Don't let the king thing go to your head. You'll mess it up, same as I will. We'll both be out on our ears in no time. Mooney doesn't seem the sort to take prisoners.'

'She also doesn't seem the sort you want to get on the wrong side of,' said Ange.

'She'll soon see the error of her ways,' I answered confidently.

'Oh yeah? Look what she did to Ryan.'

'That's Ryan, this is me.'

'You don't deserve to be in the play, McCue.'

'No, you're right. I don't.' I reached for the script I'd thrown on the floor earlier. 'Here, all yours.'

She knocked it away. 'I wouldn't play that part if I was paid to.'

'But Ange, you'd be brilliant at it.'

She looked unsure if I was joking or not.

'You think?'

'Absolutely. I always say that if you ever want someone to play a bottom or an ass, it's Angie Mint.'

She leapt on me, snarling. Some people have no sense of humour.

35

CHAPTER FOUR

The last two days of the week went by without much happening except one boring lesson after another and threat after threat from teachers for not paying attention, for doing something wrong, for answering back, or just for being a living, breathing, burping kid at their rotten mercy. All part of the National Curriculum of School Life. The only out-of-the-ordinary thing occurred just after Friday lunch, on the way to class. The others had gone on ahead while I paid a snap visit to the Boys. When I came out the corridor was deserted, which meant I had to get a move on. Next lesson was with Face-Ache Dakin, who doesn't hand out medals to late arrivers. I'm always telling him to relax about this. 'Sir,' I say, 'move your lessons back five minutes, or better still an hour, then we won't be so late,' but Dakin isn't huge on the Voice of Reason, specially mine.

I was approaching the corner at the end of the

corridor when I tripped. It was only a little trip, not one to Barbados or Greenland, but a trip's a trip and naturally I wondered what had made me do it as I was walking on a flat floor rather than a rocky mountain path. I looked down. My shoelace was undone. So, just before I turned the corner, I knelt down to tie the lace, hoping it wasn't wet (I'd just visited the pee-flooded urinals after all) and tied a swift double bow. Then, because my destination was the other side of the corner I was kneeling in front of, I simultaneously stood up and went round it, which you have to admit is pretty clever. Unfortunately, at that very moment someone decided to come round the corner from the opposite direction and the top of my upward-storming head slammed under that person's jutting jaw.

'Nnnnngggg!' the oncoming corner-stroller grunted.

'Oooooo!' This was me.

As I removed the peak of my head from the underbelly of the jaw, I couldn't help noticing that the Nnnnngggger was Ms Mooney, who was reeling a little. Actually we were both reeling, but her reel was probably more impressive than mine, she being a Drama teacher and all.

When she saw who it was that had jawed her without permission, her watering eyes clouded over.

'You!' she said.

'And you,' I said, hugging the McCue cranium and hoping there wasn't a crack the size of the Grand Canyon under the magnificent hairstyle. 'Wow. Corners. So dangerous. Shouldn't be allowed.'

She reeled some more, clutching her jaw, which didn't seem to amuse her even though it rhymed.

'What are you doing, charging along like that?' she demanded.

'I wasn't charging, I was doing it for free.'

'You could have hurt me! You *did* hurt me!'

'You hurt me too. And it takes two to crash.'

'Are you arguing with me, young man?'

'Arguing? No, it's just that when I open my mouth words escape.'

She fixed me with those sharp black eyes of hers.

'Do you realise that you've just assaulted a teacher?'

'I didn't assault you, I just came round a corner.

I do that quite often and I've never been accused of assault before.'

'Perhaps you've never head-butted someone before.'

'No, and I won't again if I can help it. It's painful.'

'Have you heard of the three-strikes-and-you're-out system of justice?' she asked.

'Dunno. Should I have?'

'Commit three crimes and when you're caught the third time it's life.'

'Life?'

'Imprisonment.'

'I haven't committed any crimes.'

'What you've done is upset me twice now,' she said. 'First in Drama, now here. Once more and…well, you'll see.'

'You'll lock me up?'

'Lock you up?' She smiled for the second time since we met. Like before, it wasn't the kind of smile that warms the old cockles. 'Oh no,' she said. 'That would be against the law. But annoy me one more time and believe me, you'll wish I *had* merely locked you up.'

She started to go, but stopped.

39

'And if I need dental work, your parents will be getting the bill!'

She swept away, still holding her jaw. Watching her go, I felt something trickle down my back. I think it was ice.

CHAPTER FIVE

It was Saturday morning and because we couldn't think of anything else to do, Pete, Angie and I went walkies down by the canal. The canal is one of those places we weren't allowed to go to when we were younger. Back then it was a hang out for druggies and people we weren't supposed to mix with, and there were always tin cans and beer crates and other junk floating in the water. We went there once when we were eight and our parents found out and tied us to chairs for a week to stop us ever wanting to go there again, but there's been a big clean-up operation down there since then. Dodgy types are banned, nothing floats on the water except dead fish, and there are flowers along the towpaths, and grassy banks where there used to be clinker and mud and unwanted bedsteads and stuff. These days you often find families strolling along hand in hand and smiling. In other words, it's become respectable, which probably means that it's no longer off limits to us, though we haven't checked with the Golden Oldies just in case.

There's even a Visitors' Car Park above the canal now. This bit of ground used to be a bomb site, minus bombs. When it was a bombless bomb site you didn't have to pay to park your car there, but now that it's an official car park you do, and there's a ticket meter, and an inspector to fine you if you're there longer than you thought you'd be, so someone does well out of it. Fortunately, we didn't have a car to get a ticket and fine for, and so far they haven't found a way to fine people for just having feet, so we turned them towards the steps down to the canal. As we approached the steps, two men in overalls came up them and threw some gear into a blue and yellow van, which we hoped was theirs. They were chuckling about some work they'd just done somewhere below.

'Well, she wanted a good strong spring and that's what she's got, so she can't blame us if the worst happens,' one of the men said.

'You'd have to weigh at least twelve stone to keep it down,' said the other man. 'She can't weigh more than eight or nine. It could flip right up when she turns over.'

'Let's hope for her sake that she's not a tosser and turner then.'

'I hope she is,' said the second man. 'Bad-tempered cow.'

There was a good view of the canal from the steps. Boats moored along it and all. Nice sight. It must be great to live on a boat. You don't have to stay in the same spot all the time, unlike a house. I wake up and go to my window some mornings and wish with all my might that the view will be different when I open the curtains, but it never is. If you lived on a boat you could be somewhere else every day. I like the sound of that.

We were nearly at the bottom of the steps when we realised the two men had also started down again. When we reached the towpath we started walking, and so did they when they reached it. We stopped, pretending to look at one of the boats, thinking they would go by, but they didn't. They climbed onto the boat and went inside.

'Weird boat,' I said, looking it over.

It was wider than any of the others along the

43

bank, with a high back end, like an extra floor had been added inside. It was also very brightly painted – yellow, orange and red. Made your eyes hurt.

'It's a converted Dutch barge,' Angie said.

'How would you know that?'

'I know it,' she said, 'because last term we did a project on inland waterway craft. All of us, including you two.'

Pete and I shrugged at one another. There are some things that are worth forgetting even before you hand the work in, and this sounded like one of them.

'What's Dutch about it?' Pete asked.

'They used to be made in Holland,' Angie said.

'Long way to come from Holland,' I said.

'That's the beauty of water, McCue. Boats float on it.'

'If I had a boat I wouldn't feel safe parking it on a canal,' Pete said. 'I mean look, they're only tied. S'pose the ropes got loose. You could stick your head up on deck one morning and find you're in the middle of the ocean.'

Just then, the two men came up from below and

jumped over the side. Fortunately for them, the side they jumped over was the one with land attached to it.

'Hey, look at the name of this thing,' Angie said. 'The *Katherine Hamlet*. There's a Shakespeare play called *Hamlet*.'

I growled. 'The next person to say that name before next Wednesday gets thumped.'

'What, *Hamlet*?'

'Shakespeare.'

She thumped me.

We walked on.

Then Pete said: 'I've been looking at my script. Bits of it are quite interesting.'

'Yes,' I said. 'The bits that say "The" and "End".'

'No, I mean the way the characters talk. Pretty loopy, but—'

'Forget it, I don't want to hear about it.'

'OK, but—'

I held my hand up. 'Garrett. Stop. No more.'

He shut up.

We were some way along the towpath when we heard a voice behind us.

'You men! Just a minute!'

As you might have guessed, this wasn't aimed at us. But we knew the voice.

'I don't believe it,' I said.

We gaped as Ms Mooney clambered off the Dutch barge and leapt up the steps after the men.

'Give me a lift to the shopping centre,' she said. It sounded more like an order than a request. 'Save me getting my bike out.'

'Gotta rearrange the gear on the van before we go,' one of them answered, obviously hoping the delay would put her off.

'I can wait,' Ms M said. 'If you're quick.'

The men finished the climb up the steps with unhappy shoulders. Miss followed them and soon they and she were out of sight.

'*She* lives on a *boat*?' Angie said incredulously.

'Dutch barge,' I said.

'Yes, but a teacher living on the canal, who'd have thought it?'

'I wonder how you sink a boat?' said Pete. We turned to him. 'Well, why not?' he said. 'We don't like her, do we?'

'You'd need dynamite or a depth charge or something,' I said. 'All I've got in my pocket is an elastic band and some gum.'

'We could untie the ropes. Be a laugh to see it drift away.'

'Tempting,' I murmured, picturing it.

'Not for me,' said Angie. 'I'm not into vandalism.'

'It's not vandalism,' I said. 'Vandalism's smashing things up. We'd just be untying a couple of ropes.'

'And if you're seen?'

Pete and I looked up and down the canal. The nearest boat was moored some way along and there was no one on its deck. No one on the path either.

'You up for it?' Pete said to me.

I nodded. 'Yeah. The old battleaxe deserves it.'

'OK, I'm gone,' said Angie.

'You're leaving us to do it on our own?' said Pete.

'Bet your little cotton socks I am.'

'But Ange,' I said. 'We're the Three Musketeers. If two of us do something, so does the third.'

'Not this time she doesn't. I want no part of setting boats adrift.'

And she walked away. Not back up the steps. Along the towpath.

'Ange!' I shouted.

She didn't stop, didn't turn.

'Let her go,' said Pete. 'Who needs a girl around at a time like this?'

'Yeah, but Ange isn't like a girl, she's...Ange.'

'Still don't need her. This is man's work.'

I looked at the ropes that tethered the barge to the bank. One at the back end, one at the front. Two ropes, two of us.

'Yeah, who needs her?'

After one more left-right-left glance to make sure there were no lurking observers in dark glasses and camouflaged clothing, Pete got to work on the rope at the back while I started on the front one. He got his untied quicker than I did mine.

'You always were useless with knots,' he said, rejoining me.

'It must be tighter than yours,' I snapped.

'No, you don't know what you're doing, is all. Want me to show you?'

'No!'

'So struggle. I'm going to look at that green one along there.'

'Green what?'

'Boat. I can see myself on one like that. I'd wear a cap and have a parrot that swore.'

He ambled off to eyeball the green boat. Angie wasn't on the path ahead of him any more. Must have left it by some other steps further on. I went back to my thankless task. It really wasn't easy, but I managed it. And just as I got it free…

'Talk about caught in the act!'

My hands froze. I turned, slowly, frozen hands in front of me like a squirrel gripping its nuts.

'I… I… I…'

'Yes?' said Miss Mooney.

'I thought you'd gone to the shops.'

'I wonder where you were when I announced *that* intention? Hiding, no doubt, waiting for me to go. But since you're so interested, I came back for my purse. Just as well I did, it seems. Retie that rope please, before she moves away.'

'I was tying it,' I lied. 'It looked loose. I was doing you a favour.'

'Oh yes? And how do you explain the stern rope? Is that also loose through no intervention on your part?'

I started retying my rope and she marched to the back of the boat, got down on her knees, leant out over the water. While she grabbed and reknotted

49

the stern rope I looked along the path towards the green boat. No sign of Pete.

Mooney came back and snatched my rope – 'Give me that!' – and fixed it while I stood by helplessly, wondering what was coming. 'So, Jiggy McCue!' she said, rising to her full small height.

'It was just a lark,' I said. No point trying to worm my way out of it any more. Couldn't say I'd had an accomplice either. I would have, but my accomplice had vamoosed, so she probably wouldn't have believed me.

'A lark,' she repeated. 'Setting my home adrift. Yes, I see what fun that must have seemed to you. To *me*, though, it's yet another personal attack, this time on my property. Remember what I said about three strikes? This latest transgression – the last one has earned me a dental appointment, by the way – brings you swiftly to the third strike, which results in...' She leant towards me, eyes gleaming darkly. '*Punishment.*'

I held my hands up. 'I apologise, Miss. Stupid thing to do. I deserve to be sacked from the play. OK, that's fair, I don't blame you.'

'Sack you from the play?' she said. 'But that

would be what you want. No, no, I'm thinking of something else entirely. A special something, just for you, to go with the part.'

'Go with the part?' I said nervously.

Her eyes went even darker suddenly. 'Bottom,' she said.

And all at once I felt like I was being drawn into the dark core of her eyes. Drawn and drawn and drawn, and then I was falling – felt like it anyway – down a deep black pit with nothing to hold onto, nothing at all, and—

'Jig? Jig!'

'Uh?'

I was sitting on the top step above the canal.

'What are you doing?' said Angie.

'I...dunno.'

I got up. How had I got here? Where had the time gone?

'What happened with Mooney?' Pete asked. 'I saw her coming back down the steps and skipped. Caught up with Ange and we came back another way. You in the deep stuff?'

'I...dunno,' I said again.

I didn't feel dizzy or anything, just confused.

51

What had happened? How had I got from standing in front of Ms Mooney on the towpath to the top of the steps without knowing anything about it?

We started across the car park. A four-by-four pulled in from the slip road that led up to it. The driver parked and got out. So did a woman in the passenger seat, and two little kids in the back.

'Hi,' the man said as we drew level with them.

'Hi,' said Angie.

Angie's far too friendly with strangers. Pete never is. I am sometimes, but I didn't feel like talking right now. I paused though. Didn't plan to, but I had to. The man and woman gaped at me.

'What?' I asked them.

Before they could tell me, Angie grabbed my arm, said 'Sorry, sorry, sorry,' and hurried me away while Pete did something with my belt.

'Geddoff, what are you doing?!' I said, batting him away.

'What am *I* doing?' he said.

'Jig, what just got into you?' Angie demanded.

'What the hell are you talking about?'

'I'm talking about what you did in front of that family, what else?'

'I didn't do anything.'

'Oh, you call dropping your pants and giving them a grandstand view nothing, do you?'

'I what?'

'Waved your bare backside at them.'

'I didn't.'

'You did. You know you did.'

I didn't deny it again because I knew, deep down, way down in the dark pit Miss Mooney had cast me into as a special punishment, that I'd done exactly what Angie said. I'd mooned, to a family of total strangers, without wanting to, meaning to, knowing I was doing it.

And so it all started.

CHAPTER SIX

I stayed in for the rest of the day. All Sunday too. Swoozie was the only person I talked to apart from my parents. I told her more than them, of course, because she understood me and they didn't. Mum thought I'd fallen out with Pete and Angie. I let her think what she liked. Fact was I didn't dare go out in case I dropped my pants in public again without knowing it.

I might have been able to stay in at the weekend, but I couldn't on Monday. I was nervous going to school that morning. P and A were a bit nervy too. Walked a few paces away from me in case they had to pretend they'd never seen me before in their life. I didn't drop anything again, though, and once at school, where the day's lessons quickly turned my brain to processed cheese triangles, I stopped even thinking about the possibility.

Afternoon came, and History with Hurley. Every year they reshuffle the lessons so they fall on different days to confuse us, but they don't reshuffle the teachers, so we're always stuck with the same old has-beens, like Mr H, whose lesson is never a bucketful of laughs. His subject today was Elizabethan England. Elizabethan England? What did that have to do with us? If he *had* to tell us about some bit of the dead and buried past, why couldn't he do the Wild West, or Roman battles, or The Great Teletubby Massacre of 1242 or something? As usual in Hurley's lesson, my mind wandered. Don't ask where it wandered to, I wasn't paying attention to that either, but at least I had something to look at apart from maps and posters, the backs of drooping heads, and the Snoozemeister himself. In the scramble to get the best desks that always occurs at the start of a new school year, I'd managed to get one right at the back and next to the window. Pete was narked about the window because although I'd graciously allowed him to sit next to me yet again, he had to lean over to see past me. Not that there was much to see, even from my seat. The History room's on the ground floor, so you don't get romantic vistas of sweeping hills and so on. You get other parts of

55

the school and the teachers' car park. Still, you take what's on offer in lessons like Hurley's, and I was gazing out there while he droned on and on, until he said a name that caught my ear and made me groan out loud without meaning to. The droning stopped.

'Sorry, was there something at the back there?'

No one owned up until Ryan the wonder dog barked the info.

'It was McCue. He groaned.'

I snarled at him. He smirked back.

'Why did you groan, Mr McCue?' Hurley asked.

'It's Shakespeare, sir.'

'What about him?'

'I've heard all I want to about him for the next three hundred years.'

'Oh, have you? Sorry, didn't know that.'

'That's OK, sir, you're only doing your sad excuse for a job.'

'Shakespeare was a prominent figure in the last decade or so of Elizabeth's reign,' he said.

'That a fact,' I said. 'Fascinating. Next subject.'

'He wrote some of his finest plays before her death in 1603.'

'Wow.'

'It's believed that the queen saw one or more of them. That he might even have been commissioned to write one for her.'

'Terrific. Now, moving on…'

And on he went, and on and on and on, mostly about Billy-Bob Shake-a-leg, just to annoy me. I hunched down behind the heads in front and turned to the window again. And who should I see dismounting from her multicoloured bike but my new least-favourite teacher, Ms Mooney. As she strung a chain round some spokes she glanced my way, and when she saw me she rose, eyes fixed on mine. I would have looked away or closed my peepers, but for one thing.

I couldn't.

She had me in another eye-lock from which there was no escape.

'Jig, zip it.'

I jumped. Pete, in my ear. I blinked. Looked at him.

'Zip it?'

'The mouth. You're muttering.'

'I'm not.'

'Are. A bunch of olden-style mumbly-jumbly.'

I asked him what he was talking about. At least, I thought I did. But the room fell silent the moment I said it, and everyone, including Mr H, was staring at me.

'Did you just use a four-letter word in my class, Mr McCue?' Hurley asked.

'Er…probably. I use a lot of those.'

'You do?'

'Sure. Crab, deli, spit, plum, nuts, you name it, I probably say it.'

'Which one was it that you said to Garrett?'

I shrugged. 'Sorry, don't have a written transcript.'

'He called him a rancid quat, sir.' This was Julia Frame.

'Thank you, Julia,' said Mr Hurley.

'Pleasure, sir.'

'I didn't say that,' I said. 'Why would I say… what was it?'

'Rancid quat,' Julia said.

'Once is enough, Julia,' said Hurley. 'See me after class, McCue. We have a detention to talk about.'

'Oh, you can't give him a detention for that, sir.' Julia again.

Hurley frowned at her. Julia was usually so quiet. Most of the time you wouldn't know she was there, or miss her if she wasn't.

'I certainly *can* give someone a detention for uttering an obscenity in my class,' Hurley said.

'It's not an obscenity, sir, it's Shakespeare, the person you were telling us about.'

'Shakespeare?'

'Othello. Act 5, Scene 1, I think. Iago to Roderigo. "I have rubb'd this young quat almost to the sense, and he grows angry." It means pimple, sir.'*

'Pimple?'

'Yes. I think Jiggy's just entering into the spirit of what you're teaching us. That's not a bad thing, is it?'

'Well, no, but…' Hurley shook his head, firmed up his chunky jaw and tried to retake control of the situation. 'But I will *not* have people talking in my class!'

'You do,' said Ryan.

'Detention, Ryan!'

'Now that's just *mean*,' Ryan said.

---

* Only Julia would know *any* of that!

'Double detention!'

Ryan jumped up and glared across at me. 'I'll get you for this, McCue!'

I glared back. 'Away with you, thou codpiece-sniffing pignut!'

'What?' he said.

'An arrant clod such as thee is not worthy of the spit upon my lip.'

'*What!*'

Now I stood up. 'Seal thy ugly hole, thou rump-fed scut!'

'McCue! Enough!'

This was Mr Hurley. I turned to him. I didn't want to. Had to, no choice. And I had to speak.

'Thou dost intrude, thou ancient droning flap-mouth!'

Now it was his turn to say 'What?', only when he said it, it was more like 'WHAT???!!!'

But I was on a roll. My mouth was anyway.

'Art thy ears made of cloth, O gnat-headed dolt?'

'Jig.'

Pete. In my ear. I turned to him.

'Leave me be, thou onion-eyed puttock!'

'Hey, come on,' he said, 'I'm on your side.'

'My side needs not the faith of such a weedy mouldwarp!'

'McCue! Out of my class! Now!' Hurley bawled.

I didn't need bawling twice. Out of there seemed a fine place to be right then. Fortunately, my legs were still on my payroll even if my trap wasn't. I aimed them at the door.

'I depart, O fool-born dotard!' I chirruped.

'Jig, be *quiet*!'

This was Angie as I passed her desk. I would have bad-mouthed her too, but she leapt up, clamped my lips between a thumb and forefinger (hers) and strong-armed me to the door. Then she shoved me outside. And the moment we were in the corridor...

'Ange,' I said, jerking my lips from her grasp.

'Don't say it!' she said fiercely. 'I will *not* be insulted by you!'

'No, no,' I protested. 'It's over. It's gone.'

'What's over, what's gone?'

'The need to say all that stuff. I couldn't help it. Mooney made me. It had to be her. Where else would I get old-time garbage like that?'

'I never know with you. What do you mean, Mooney made you?'

'She hypnotised me.'

'Hypnotised you?'

'Or something. Just before I started spewing all that stuff I saw her outside, and next thing I knew—'

The door opened. Hurley's head bounced out, all red and bloated. His neck spilled over his tight collar like it had an ambition to explode.

'Angie Mint, in here! McCue, go to Mr Hubbard's office and wait for me! I'll be along in a minute when I finish here!'

'Look, sir,' I said. 'Sorry about all that, it wasn't—'

'SAVE IT FOR THE HEAD! GO!'

I wenteth.

CHAPTER SEVEN

While I was waiting in Miss Prince's office (the scented airlock between the Head's office and the rest of the school) I decided how I would handle the situation when I stood in front of Mother Hubbard's desk. Previous interviews with our beloved Head had taught me that the best thing to do when you're up before him is to tell a believable lie and look sincere while you do it – and that's what I did when Mr Hurley arrived. I based this version on something Julia had said in the classroom.

'I was out of order, sir. Mr Hurley was talking about Shakespeare, and as we're doing a Shakespeare play with Ms Mooney and I've been studying the script really hard, I thought he – Mr H – would be quite impressed that I'd got a handle on how they spoke back then.'

'Don't give me that!' Hurley spluttered. 'You were using insulting language!'

'The language of Shakespeare,' I said innocently. 'Didn't mean to upset you, sir, really I didn't.'

'Didn't mean to *upset* me?' he bellowed. 'Didn't mean to *upset* me?'

'No, sir. Sorry if you took it the wrong way. I won't say a word in your class ever again – promise.'

It worked. With Hubbard anyway. When Hurley demanded my head on a cracked dinner plate, Mother, bless him, let me off with a gentle warning – 'Save the Shakespeare talk for Ms Mooney's lesson, there's a good lad' – and dismissed me. As I closed the door super-quietly behind me, Hurley was still fuming and taking my name in vain, but I didn't care. I was off the hook and swimming out to sea, so the boring old quat (as in pimple) could rant till the cows came home for cocoa.

Out in the playground Julia came up to me. Her eyes were shining.

'Jiggy, I didn't know you knew so much Shakespeare!' she gushed.

'Makes two of us,' I confessed.

'Makes four of us,' said Angie as she and Pete joined us.

'It was pretty cool actually,' said Pete, which was really something coming from him.

'The way it rolled out of him!' Julia said. 'And *such* words!' she added with a sickening sigh.

'They were insults, Julia,' said Angie.

'But *Shakespearean* insults. I couldn't say which plays most of them came from, but it was wonderful to hear such language.'

'Hurley didn't think so.'

'Jiggy,' Julia said, cosying up to me in a worrying sort of way.

I flattened my hands on my chest. Nearest I could get to an anti-Frame defence shield. 'Mm?'

'Can I be your understudy?'

'My understudy?'

'In *A Midsummer Night's Dream*.'

'A Midsummer Nightmare for me,' I said.

'Can I?'

'Jools,' I said. 'I'm playing a plonker called Bottom. You really want to understudy my Bottom?'

'Oh, yes!' she said. 'If I understudied you, and you were taken ill on the day of the performance, I could stand in for you.'

'Stand in for me?'

'Take your place.'

'Take my place…'

I mulled this over. But not for long. Almost at once a plan unfurled. If I couldn't get out of rehearsals but came over all faint on the big day, Mooney would have to let me off the actual show. Then Julia could wear the ass's head instead of me. The fact that she was short and dumpy and I was not wouldn't matter. This was acting after all, and because she was so keen she was bound to put a lot more into her Bottom than I would into mine.

'You might have to ask Mooney,' I said. 'But it's dandy with…me…'

I'd noticed someone watching from one of the windows. Ms Mooney herself. She was giving me that look again. That really dark look.

'Jig, why are you unbuckling your belt?' Angie asked.

'My belt?'

I looked down. I was unbuckling my belt. I carried on watching – we all did – as I unzipped my trousers and ankled them.

'Jiggy, what…?' Julia gasped, backing away.

'My question exactly,' said Pete, though he stayed put.

They were staring at the Iron Man logo on the front of my exposed underpants. I turned my back to them, not in embarrassment or to cover my gusset, but to yank my undies down.

'Why do boys *do* that?' some girl said as I waggled my bare bum.

'Because they're from Mars, where lobotomies are free,' said another.

'Pete!' Angie hissed. 'Cover him!'

She and Pete slammed their shoulders together and tried to make themselves as obese as possible in front of my behind. They were still jostling for space when my hands suddenly felt like they belonged to me again. I tested them by reaching down and gripping my pants. I was able to haul them up. And my trousers. And zip them, and rebuckle the belt. Respectable again, I turned round.

'Where's Julia?' I asked.

'The bike sheds, probably,' said Ange. 'Hiding from the likes of you.'

'Understudies,' said Pete. 'First sign of a script change and they're off.'

67

I glanced up at the windows. Mooney was still there, smiling cruelly.

'Let's get out of here,' I said, and marched round the corner to the sanctuary of the Concrete Garden. 'Did you see her?' I asked, throwing myself on a bench.

'Who?'

'Mooney. She made me flash my bass drum in public again.'

'You really think she's behind it?' said Pete.

I frowned at him. 'This is no time for your stupid jokes, Garrett.'

'Jokes, what jokes?'

'"Behind it".'

He grinned. 'Hey, I do it without even thinking!'

'I can't believe Miss made you do it,' Angie said. 'She's just a teacher. Teachers don't have abilities like that. All they're trained to do is stand in front of us and bore the pants off us.'

'Well, she's obviously got a degree in *that*,' I said. 'Look, I know it's her. She made me spew all those Neolithic insults and flash the flesh – twice now – because I made fun of her name the day we met, and because I headed her jaw, and—'

'Headed her jaw?' said Pete. (I hadn't told them about that.)

'—and because she caught me freeing her boat. She can make me do anything she wants!'

They looked at one another. Then they looked back at me. They had nothing to offer. This was starting to look like one of those deals the Musketeers couldn't help with. It was me against Mooney. Just me. Solo.

CHAPTER EIGHT

Julia might have changed her mind about standing in for my Bottom, but at our second Wednesday Drama session Ms Mooney announced that everyone had to learn all the lines of all the parts, so that…

'If, at the very last minute, one of my cast has to drop out for some reason – though woe betide them if they do! – there'll be no shortage of others to step into his or her place.'

Once again, she'd read my mind.

It was our first read-through of the script. We actors had to read our parts out loud and the rest of the class had to read along with us, but silently. I'm terrible at reading aloud, always have been, and I wasn't the only one, but Mooney didn't complain. Said all she wanted for now was for us to get a feel for the words. Oh, we got a feel for them all right.

We'd been reading for about twenty minutes when Mrs Mahendra, a teacher who took us for nothing, looked in.

'Ophelia,' she said. 'Call for you in the office.'

Ms Mooney spun round. 'I'm in a lesson!' she snapped.

Mrs Mahendra jumped. 'I'm only passing it on. Miss Prince says it's Equity.'

An instant change came over Mooney. The how-dare-you-interrupt-me-when-I'm-working fierceness vanished in a twitch. She looked almost pleased as she turned to the class.

'Would anyone here call themselves responsible?'

Three hands went up. All girls'.

'You three are in charge while I'm away. I want you to ensure that the read-through continues. Any tomfoolery will be dealt with on my return. And believe me...' – she glared round – '...you don't want to get on my bad side.' The glare rested on me a second or two longer than anyone else.

There was a slight pause after she went, then the three who'd been put in charge got together and told us to carry on. One of the boys gently suggested they pay a visit to a taxidermist, but then someone started to say their lines, and although there was a spot of background chatter, others took their turns and the reading continued.

I scanned the nearest bits of my dialogue. I wasn't due to speak for a page and a half, so I could relax for a bit. Angie saw this too and came over.

'Equity?' she said. 'Isn't that the actors' union?'

'How would I know?'

'Maybe she's an actress and they've got a job for her.'

'She's already got a job. Getting me a bad rep.'

'You had one of those before she came along.'

'How about her name then!' This was Pete, joining us. 'Ophelia. A-feel-ya, A-feel-ya. Wah-hoo.'

'I thought her name might be Katherine,' Angie said.

'Why Katherine?' I asked.

'Name of her boat.'

'I can't remember the name of her boat.'

'The *Katherine Hamlet*. I remember it because of the Hamlet, like in the play. Did Hamlet have a wife? Or a daughter?'

'Dunno, I'm still struggling with *Beast Quest*. Ask Julia.'

'No need. Come over here.'

She led us away from the others and tugged something out of her pocket. A BlueBerry.

72

'You'll be lynched if you're caught using that in a lesson,' said Pete.

'Yeah, well.' Angie tapped some buttons. I asked her what she was doing. 'Seeing if there's a Katherine in *Hamlet*,' she said.

'*Hamlet*. That's not the one where the king talks to a skull, is it?'

'Think so,' she said.

'Just as well we're not doing that then. Mooney'd make me play the skull.'

'Bingo!'

'What?'

'Holy Shmoly.'

'Are you gonna keep this to yourself, or...?'

'It says here that when Shakespeare was in his teens a woman called Katherine Hamlet drowned in the river he lived near, and there's a strong possibility that he based the character of Ophelia on her in *Hamlet* the play, when he wrote it years later.'

'A-feel-ya,' Pete chuckled. 'A-feel-ya.'

'In the play, Ophelia drowns,' said Ange. 'Sounds like *our* Ophelia – Ms Mooney – identifies with poor drowned Katherine. That could be why

73

she lives on the water, named her boat after her, and is mad about Shakespeare.'

'She's just mad,' I said.

'Bottom!'

I jumped. The entire class was looking my way. I glanced down. No, I hadn't done it again. 'What?' I said.

'You're supposed to come in here,' said Hislop.

'Come in what?'

He rattled his script.

'Oh, that.' I went back to where I'd been standing before Miss left. 'Where are we?'

'Page 14, line 5.'

I found the page and line and had just started when Mooney returned. She didn't look half as happy as when she left, so I guessed that whatever happened on the phone with Equity hadn't worked out the way she hoped.

'That's dreadful!' she said to me almost at once.

It was on the tip of my tongue to say that I thought she didn't care how it sounded as this was just a read-through, but I didn't want to risk anything. She told me to read my lines again, and I did.

'"There are things in this comedy that will never please. First I must draw a sword and kill myself."'

'Go for it, Bottom!' said Ryan.

I snarled at him. 'Shut it, Fairy Pukeblossom.'

'Peaseblossom, be silent,' Ms Mooney said. 'Continue, Bottom.'

'I'm done,' I said. 'It's Quince next.'

'Go on then, Quince, say your piece.'

Aziz said Quince's piece, then it was back to me, then a couple of others, then the scene changed and I could breathe again. I really *hate* reading out loud in public. Pete does too usually, but for once he didn't do half badly. Miss must have thought so too because she said that he did pretty well for a first reading. Pete looked like she'd offered him a knighthood.

CHAPTER NINE

I'm going to skip on a bit now because most of what happened in the next few weeks is just too yawnworthy to write about.* Ms Mooney carried on making me do stuff I wouldn't normally do whenever I said or did something she didn't like, and sometimes when I'd done nothing except glance her way. Unfortunately, her favourite thing went on being me flashing the old bumeroonie. After its second public outing I knew when I was doing it, but knowing wasn't a huge bonus as I still couldn't stop myself. That wasn't the only thing, though. She also made me backchat teachers more than usual, write rude words on the boards of empty classrooms, and draw hair, specs and horns on the staff that hang outside the Head's office (their photos, I mean).

Apart from all this it was mostly business as usual. Here are some of the highs and lows of the weeks I can't be bothered to tell you about.

---

* This is a school term I'm talking about, not crossing the Himalayas on stilts dressed as Jemima Puddleduck.

1. I got five detentions, my record for half a term. Three of these were for things mentioned above. The other two were from Mr Rice for not bringing my boots in on a footie day (I said they'd been run over by a milk float, but he didn't believe me) and from Face-Ache Dakin, who likes to give me at least one per half term, whether I deserve it or not.

2. I caught a cold, or rather a cold caught me, and had two legitimate days off school (best days of the entire half term).

3. Mrs Gamble gave me a prize in English. It was for an essay about where we lived. I stretched the brief a bit and wrote about life on Borderline Way, where we lived before we moved to the Brook Farm Estate. The prize was a little book about sticklebacks. I didn't ask what sticklebacks had to do with a street that'd been flattened since I lived there. I'd never been given anything at school before except the odd star, and I was so pathetically grateful that I even read the book.*

4. Ms Mooney gave me the bill for her dental treatment. She said that either I had to pay it or my parents did. Well, *I* couldn't. I didn't get that

---

* You could ask me anything about sticklebacks now, but no one ever does, can't think why.

much pocket money in six months. I took it to my dad.

'What's this?'

'Dental bill from one of my teachers.'

'Why are you giving it to me?'

'I head-butted her. Dislodged one of her teeth, she says.'

'You head-butted a teacher?'

'Yes.'

'Jig, you can't go round head-butting teachers.' He looked at the bill again. 'It's too expensive.'

'I only did it once.'

'Oh, good. Hate to think it was a new hobby.' He handed the bill back. 'Give it to your mother.'

Apart from these things it was just tons of school work, tons of homework, tons of boredom, and the rotten play. We met in the gym every Wednesday afternoon to read and act bits of the script, and when we weren't there we were expected to spend every waking minute memorising our parts. Most of us didn't get any better at acting, mainly because we didn't want to be in the play. Atkins was the worst of all. Even when he had just one line and said it over and over again he got it wrong, but

Miss wouldn't let anyone take over from us, however lousy we were.

'The idea is to see how you *develop*,' she said, 'not give up on you just because you're patently dreadful and unlikely *ever* to improve.'

Really knew how to boost your confidence, that woman.

The only real surprise was Pete. Pete's never been the slightest cop at English, doesn't like to read, can't spell for toffee-apples, but once he got into the ancient guff of Shakespeare something totally un-Garrett came over him. He attended after-school rehearsals without his arm twisted behind his back, and often we'd be strolling along out of school and he'd be quothing his lines in different ways to see which sounded best. This usually ended with me and Ange thumping him or walking away with our hands over our ears, but he wasn't put off. I reckoned it was Mooney bending him to her will. Angie wasn't so sure.

'You know Pete,' she said. 'Once he gets into something he doesn't let go till he's rigor-mortised everyone around. Remember the dinosaur fixation? He knew the names of every species and what they

79

had for breakfast. And the cars period? Talked about nothing but the different makes and models, their revs and zero-to-sixty speeds and all the rest for six months nonstop. Now it's this play. It'll pass.'

'You think?'

'If it doesn't I'll have to kill him.'

One Saturday Angie called for me. She was wearing new sunglasses. Reflective silver wraparounds. I leant towards her and peered at my two gleaming faces.

'Hey, I'm twice as handsome in these.'

She pushed me away. 'Let's go somewhere.'

'Where?'

'Anywhere.'

I looked over her shoulder at the day behind her. 'Bit bright.'

'That's why I'm wearing these. Bring yours, then you won't moan all the time.'

'Can't. Broken. Dad sat on them.'

'Why, couldn't he find a chair?'

'Hang on, think I saw Mum's in the kitchen.'

I went to the kitchen and found my mother's

sunglasses. They were huge. She'd been wearing them ever since she got her first part with the am-dram group, like she was the star (she was the maid in an old-fashioned comedy about people who play tennis all the time). I put the glasses on and groped my way back to the front step. They had very dark lenses indoors.

'You look like a girl,' Angie said.

'You can talk,' I said. 'Going out!' The last bit was a shout, for the house. It didn't answer, so I closed the door behind me. 'What's Pete doing?' I asked as we headed for the gate.

'Driving me up the wall.'

'Why this time?'

'Sprinz and Aziz are round. They're going over their lines together. Loudly.'

'How's the prop-making and stitch-work coming along?' I asked. 'I haven't checked it out lately, mainly cos I'm not interested.'

'Well as you're not interested I won't tell you. But it's looking pretty good, considering.'

'Considering what?'

'That we're all crap at making stuff.'

We mooched to the shopping centre for

somewhere to go. Good move as it turned out, because of something bad that happened as we were strolling through the arcade where all the hippy-type shops were.

'Hey, you two.'

The voice of no one we knew. But turning we saw that it was Toklas from our class. Toklas has a nickname, Sound Effects, because he's always doing funny voices and noises. He's good at imitating other people too, including famous ones.

'What's happening?' he asked, in his normal voice this time.

'Not a lot. You?'

'Same.' He clocked my mother's sunglasses. 'You look like a girl.'

'It's my new image.'

'Not rehearsing then?'

'Nah. Better things to do.'

'Yeah, me too.'

His eyes drifted over my shoulder as he said this, but as they also stayed in his head I didn't follow them. When he ducked down suddenly I didn't ask about that either. You get used to Toklas messing

82

about. We weren't even surprised when he dodged into the doorway of the sports shop we were standing outside. Ange and I were about to walk when a loud voice rang out – Toklas's, though it didn't sound like his.

'Hey, there's that mad old bag Mooney!'

Then he gave us the thumbs up and backed into the shop.

'Ah. Yes. Had to be you, didn't it?'

We turned. Ms Mooney. Glaring at me.

'Hi, Miss,' Angie said brightly, switching her best 'Good to see you' face on.

But Miss only had eyes for me.

'So that's what you think of me.'

'Sorry?' I said.

'Mad old bag Mooney. Is that a special nickname you have for me?'

'No, that wasn't me, it was Toklas, he went into that shop.'

She smiled grimly. 'You think I don't know your voice, do you?'

'Well obviously you don't,' I said. She might be a teacher, but we weren't on school premises now.

'It did sound like you, Jig,' Angie said.

'Get away. I don't sound like that.'

'You do since your voice broke.'

'Perhaps it's time for another lesson,' Ms Mooney said.

'Sorry,' I said. 'School's out.'

But her eyes were darkening. I could see this even from behind the lenses of my mother's huge sunglasses. I groaned. What would she make me do *this* time?

But nothing happened.

Mooney seemed as surprised about this as I was.

'What have you done?' she said.

'Done? Me? Nothing.'

I took off my glasses and put them in my pocket. I don't know why I did this. Maybe because it wasn't that bright in the arcade. Maybe because I suddenly felt a prat in my mother's sunglasses. Mooney's eyes were still that deepest of blacks, glaring into mine. She was pretty mad that her thing hadn't worked for once.

'Jig.'

I glanced at Angie. 'Uh?'

She looked down. So did I. My hands were doing things I hadn't told them to.

'Yes!' said Ms Mooney. 'Had me worried there for a minute.'

She flipped around and mingled with the crowd as I dropped my jeans and underpants and stuck my back end under the nose of an old lady in a wheelchair. The woman was still shouting as Angie dragged me into the distance at a fast shuffle, togs round my ankles, one hand over my front, the other over my exhaust.

But I'd just learnt something. Something well worth knowing.

'Ange!' I said as we cleared the shopping centre and I covered my personals again. 'It's the glasses! Her power doesn't work through dark glasses! You know what this means, don't you?'

'Er...'

'It means she can't make me do stuff when I'm wearing shades!'

'You think that's it?'

'Absolutely!'

'All right, but you can't wear sunglasses at school. Specially your mother's.'

'Watch me.'

From that day on, I took those glasses to school,

85

plus everywhere else in case I bumped into Mooney. I didn't actually wear them in school, but I kept a hand on the pocket they were stowed in so I could whip them out if she appeared.

'Hands out of pockets please, Jiggy.'

'I've only got one hand in one pocket, sir.'

'Well take it out, there's a good chap.'

'I can't. Got this sprained wrist. The pocket supports it.'

'OK. Good excuse.'

That was one of the nicer teachers. There are a few at Ranting Lane.

A couple of times when I saw Mooney coming I slapped the glasses on before she could get too close. I was with a bunch of others the first time and she didn't notice me, but she did the second, and frowned as she walked by. She frowned again when I wore them to the next Wednesday afternoon Drama period.

'Remove those things, Jiggy, you're not on holiday.'

'Sorry, Miss, gotta keep 'em on, quack's orders.'

The frown deepened. 'On what basis?'

'Sensitive eyes. Must keep them covered.'

'Is this a new condition?'

'Yeah. I'm having tests to try and get to the *bottom* of it.'

I smirked as I said *'bottom'* and she didn't like it one bit.

It wasn't till the next evening rehearsal that she realised why I was wearing the glasses and what it meant. She'd seen me without them earlier, at a distance, and noticed me put them on as I went in to rehearsal. She took me aside.

'What are you playing at?'

'Er...Bottom the weaver?'

'You know what I mean. Take those glasses off.'

I shook my head. 'Sorry.'

She leant towards me. 'You really are a *very* slow learner, aren't you, Jiggy?'

I knew what that meant. I was going to get another of her special lessons. But not just then. She didn't want everyone realising it was she who made me do stuff. A bit of time passed. She was nowhere near me when her black stare caught my eye across the room. My skin prickled when I saw it. Maybe I'd got it wrong and her failure at the arcade had been a freak and nothing to do with sunglasses. I felt myself gripped by her glare behind the dark lenses and expected the worst, but...nothing happened. I took a long slow breath. I'd been right. I saw it dawning on Miss that the glasses were blocking her. She stormed over.

'Take those things off right now!'

I smiled. 'Not a chance.'

She lowered her voice. 'You know, much better and brighter people than you have crossed me and lived to regret it.'

I lowered my voice too. 'Good to know I'm not alone. I'm going home now.'

'Home? You're not! You'll stay here till I say so!'

My smile broadened. I strolled towards the door whistling a tune that hadn't been written yet. The gym fell silent. I reached the door and turned, hand on knob.* All eyes were staring at me, including Mooney's pitch-black furious ones. I raised my hand in farewell and left them to it.

---

* The door's.

CHAPTER TEN

One Wednesday afternoon Ms Mooney wasn't there when we stampeded into the gym. While we were waiting for her, Hislop and Downey got into a fight, Julia Frame stamped her foot for no reason that anybody knew, and Ryan did forty-two press-ups because he's a pillock. If it hadn't been school, some of us would have left after a while, but it was, so we couldn't. Eventually, Mrs Gamble came in.

'I'll be standing in for Ms Mooney this afternoon,' she said.

'Why, Miss, is she sick?' someone asked hopefully.

'Sick?' I said. 'She's more than that. She's right off her twig.'

'All I know, and all you *need* to know,' said Mrs G, 'is that I'll be taking her place for this period. You're doing *A Midsummer Night's Dream*, I believe. Ambitious project for half a term.'

'It's a short version,' said Julia. 'It's rubbish.'

'So are they,' said Ayesha Bandari, meaning the cast (she wasn't one of us). 'And in ten days they'll be performing it. In public. It will be so *embarrassing*.'

'Oh, they can't be that bad,' said Mrs G.

'They can,' Angie assured her.

Most of us quite like Mrs Gamble, and because it was her and not Mooney even I tried to act my part better than usual. Doing the play with Mrs G was almost fun. She was complimentary about all of us too, even about Atkins mangling his Puck, which brought a big fat grin to his sad little chops – and she couldn't get over Pete.

'Peter Garrett, I had no idea you could act! You speak your lines so *well*!'

'Thanks,' Pete said, shuffling his feet. The only other time he'd ever been praised by Mrs Gamble was the time he handed in some half-decent English homework I'd knocked off for him without really trying. When she heard that the boy who played a fairy called Mustardseed was off school with food poisoning (he has school dinners), Mrs G asked if any understudy would like to take his place. Angie stuck her mitt in the air first and got the job, which cheered her up a bit.

With the end-of-half-term performance looming, Mooney had scheduled multiple rehearsals for lunchtimes and after school, but she wasn't there the following day either and Mrs Gamble couldn't do lunch, so we skipped that one. She said she would do the one that evening, though, so we trooped back to school after tea and got stuck in. When someone asked again where Mooney was, Mrs G said that no one seemed to know. There'd been no word from her.

'Anyone been to her barge?' Pete asked.

'Barge?'

'She lives on the canal.'

'I didn't know that,' Miss said. 'But I do know that Mr Hubbard sent someone to her home address, so that must have been it.'

'What happened?'

'No one in, apparently.'

As we were leaving school for the second time that day, Angie said to Pete and me, 'Let's go take a look at the *Katherine Hamlet*.'

'What for?' I said.

'To see if Ms Mooney's there, what do you think?'

'I don't want to see her. Ever.'

91

'So go home. Pete?'

He shrugged and they headed canalward. I watched them for a minute, then sighed and trudged after them. The trouble with having Three Musketeers is that you can't let Two of them go off on their own. It's hard sometimes.

Down on the towpath there was only one person in sight — a man working on a boat some way along. The green boat Pete had taken a fancy to wasn't there any more, but the *Katherine Hamlet* was, and that's the one we'd come to see, even if one of us wasn't keen. If Angie had hoped to find Mooney hanging out washing on deck she was disappointed. There was no sign of her, with or without washing.

'OK, she's not here, let's go,' I said. But Angie stepped onto the barge. 'What are you doing?' I hissed.

'What do you think I'm doing?'

'The man on that boat down there might see you.'

'So what? We're visitors.'

She knocked on the barge door. Pete and I stayed on the path while the door failed to open. Angie knocked a second time. Once again the open door plan failed miserably.

'No one home,' I said. 'Come away.'

She tried the handle, and when that didn't work went round the side and peered in a window, through her hands.

'Ange, you can't go looking in people's windows,' I said.

'She might be in there,' she replied.

'Exactly why you shouldn't look in.'

'Can't see her anyway.'

'Good. Let's get out of here.'

'Hey, this catch is loose.'

'Angie Mint, you can-*not* break in to a teacher's barge!' I hissed, sounding worryingly like my mother.

'Yes!' she crowed, jerking the window open and hoisting a leg over the sill.

'An-*gie*!' My mother's voice again.

'If you don't want to be here,' she said, half in, half out, 'then go.'

'I will,' I said, managing to speak for myself for a change. 'Coming?' I said to Pete.

'Going,' he answered – first time he'd spoken

93

since we got there – and stepped onto the deck.

'Garrett, don't be stupid! This is breaking and entering!'

'Mm. I always wanted to do that.'

He climbed in after Angie, leaving me alone and friendless on the towpath. I glanced towards the other boat. The man was looking our way. I gave a cheery wave so he wouldn't think we were doing anything we shouldn't, and stepped casually onto the barge hoping I looked like an invited guest. I waited till he turned away before flinging myself through the window, fast as a snake on steroids.

The inside of the barge was quite a surprise. I mean I know it was a boat, but a teacher lived there, so I'd kind of expected it to be sort of...teacherly. But it wasn't. There were these candles and chunky candle-holders all over the place, and incense sticks, and big beanbags, and piles of old books, and film and theatre posters, and there were fancy hats and costumes everywhere, and feather boas (scarves, not fluffy snakes), and at one end, where the boat got much higher, there was a little stage with red curtains.

The curtains were pulled back so that they hung on either side of this big painted scene of a forest. In the middle of the forest there was a figure with the head of a donkey.

'It's me!' I whispered.

Angie sighed. 'I know you think the whole world revolves around you, McCue, but it doesn't, it really doesn't.'

'Quite a coincidence, though, you have to admit.'

'Yeah, coincidence, just that. Scene from one of her fave plays, that's all.'

'You can't feel it moving,' Pete said.

I glanced his way. 'Feel what moving?'

'The boat. Barge.'

'Isn't that just as well?'

'Isn't what just as well?'

'That we can't feel it moving.'

'I thought we would, is all. As it's on water, I mean, rather than, say, concrete.'

'Jig, some books here that might interest you,' said Angie.

I joined her at the shelves of books she was standing by. Most of them were to do with the theatre, cinema or TV, but a few definitely weren't, like *The Hypnotist's Black Book*, *Secrets of Dark Eye Contact* and *How to Crucify Your Enemies*.

'This must be where she gets her...gift?' I said.

'Could be,' said Ange.

'Hey, Shakespeare!' said Pete, looking over my shoulder.

He reached for a big fat volume with *The Plays of Shakespeare* on the spine, opened it, started flipping through it.

'Photos,' Angie said. She'd moved to another part of the wall while I was still reading the spines. 'I know him,' she said. 'And him. And her. They're all actors.'

I went to the picture wall. 'Isn't that the bloke who played a wartime detective who kept crashing into trees?' I said.

'I don't remember a wartime detective who kept crashing into trees.'

'No, I mean the actor, not the tec he played. The crashes occurred when he was off-duty or whatever actors are when they're not in front of the cameras.'

'Oh yeah, that's right. Every time he went out in his car he slammed into a tree head-on. Nothing wrong with the car, he said, and he swore he wasn't on anything.'

'Look. There's a little cross on his chest.'

'A lot of people wear crosses,' Angie said.

'Not that kind. It's scratched into the photo, like with a knife.'

She peered closer. 'Woh, yeah.'

I looked at some other pictures. 'There's a cross on Helen Thingy's chest too. And James Whatsit's. And—'

'"Is this a dagger which I see before me, the handle toward my hand?",' Pete said.

We looked at him. He was reading from the Shakespeare book.

'"Come, let me clutch thee. I have thee not, and yet I see thee still. Art thou not, fatal vision, sensible to—"'

'Garrett,' Angie said.

He looked up. 'What?'

'Shut thy trap or I'll shut it for thee.'

'Hey, "Is this a dagger I see before me".' This was me.

She glared. 'Don't you start.'

'No, I mean dagger, knife, these actors. The

tree-crasher's got a cross cut into his chest like he's been dealt with. So what about the crosses on the others? Have they been dealt with too?'

We studied more photos. Crosses had been cut into other chests.

'He was in that Merlin series,' said Angie. 'He died.'

'Only in the series,' I said.

'Yes, but he fell off a horse in rehearsals and hurt his back, so they wrote him out of the show. And look, Kate Windsock or whatever her name is, bawling her eyes out at the Oscars. She was accepting an award and couldn't stop blubbing.'

'Is that a cross on her chest?'

'Yes. Dolly Fletcher's got one too.'

'Dolly Fletcher?'

'Bit-part actress, not huge, 'cept in the chest area, which she'd had pumped up. The papers called her Dolly Flasher because she kept running across football fields and cricket pitches in the altogether. She claimed her clothes kept disappearing. Everyone thought it was a publicity stunt.'

'My dad was watching a footie match on TV when she sprinted onto the pitch,' said Pete, looking up from his book. 'He was pretty annoyed.'

'Your dad was annoyed to see a nudiefied twenty-something blonde running across a football pitch?' I said in disbelief.

'No, he was annoyed because he was viewing live and couldn't watch it over and over again in slow-mo.'

Angie frowned. 'Maybe the crosses are about revenge.'

'Didn't I say that already ?' I said.

'No, you said they could mean these people have been dealt with.'

'Same thing.'

'Whatever. People "cross" her in some way, she gets back at them in *her* way, and scratches the cross on their photo. Symbolic, see.'

'She? Her? Who are we talking about?'

'Whose barge are we looking at these pictures on?' Angie said.

'You mean Mooney?'

'Of course Mooney. She's obviously into acting, and these actors have all put her back up or done her out of something, and she's learnt how to fix people who do things like that by making them

99

drive repeatedly into trees, or strip off in public, or cry buckets at award ceremonies, or fall off horses, or...or...'

She stopped. Her eyes had swollen to gobstopper size.

'Or-or?' I prompted.

'Or flash their backside and hurl insults in olden-day lingo and all the other rubbish you've been doing against your puny will.'

'Makes sense,' said Pete, shoving Shakespeare back on the shelf and drifting away.

'When Mooney's finished with you, Jig,' Angie said, 'there could be a snap of you here.'

I felt myself go pale. 'Me? Here?'

'Yes. With a cross carved into your chest. Her way of saying another one bites the dust.'

CHAPTER ELEVEN

Angie turned back to the photo wall while I was still gulping wordlessly at the scenario she'd lobbed into my mind. 'Here's that Doctor,' she said.

'Doctor?' I said, heroically managing to find my voice.

'Who. With a cross on his chest. He only played him for one series. Had to be replaced after he started beating up strangers without provocation.'

'Why would Mooney have it in for a Doctor Who?' I wondered.

'Who knows? Maybe they were auditioning for a female Doc to hang some pictures in the Tardis and she was in the running, but they gave him the part instead, so she made him bash strangers, which got him a bad press and regenerated.'

'Jig, look, it's like the one you used to have,' Pete said.

He was holding a pen. The handle was transparent. Inside it there was a man in a suit.

101

I had a sudden uncomfortable feeling.

'Tilt it,' I said.

He tilted it. The man's clothes melted away. He was starkers. Angie snatched the pen for a closer look. When she'd seen all she wanted to she held it out to me.

'Write something.'

'What for?'

'To see if it's the same as yours.'

'My pen had a female in it.'

'So this could be the male version. If it is, the result could be the same.'

'If it's one of those pens it'll only work on the person it's given to.'

'Right. And I'm giving it to you.'

'It's not yours to give, but I'm not touching it anyway. Anything printed on it?'

She screwed her eyes up. 'There's something, but I can't… Oh. Yes. Little Devils.'

'Definitely the same type then.'

'Where would Mooney get a Little Devils pen?'

'Online?' I said. 'A person with a mean agenda can get anything online.'

'Maybe she gave one of these to Dolly Fletcher

and Dolly was signing her autograph just before she ran onto the sporty venues in her birthday suit.' She tossed the pen onto a beanbag. 'Here's that smarmy soap star who came to Ranting Lane about two years ago. Looks like this was taken *at* Ranting Lane.'

She was right. It was Tony Baloney, standing on the steps down to the playground.

'Must've been taken the day he came,' I said.

'Mm. Probably by the person who scratched this cross on his chest.'

I shook my head. 'Mooney's only been at Ranting Lane since...' I clutched my forehead. 'God on a pogo stick.'

'What?'

'I just remembered where I saw her before. It was there. That day. She was the one who gave Baloney the pen he passed on to me. She meant him to sign autographs with it, so his clothes would disappear and he'd get in trouble. Her hair was different – not orange, shorter – but it was definitely her.'

'Any idea what Baloney did to upset her?'

'If I did, I've forgotten.'*

---

* To read about Jiggy's first meeting with Ms Mooney and his Little Devils pen, see *Nudie Dudie*. To hear about a certain other Little Devils product read *The Killer Underpants*. And to learn of the earliest known Little Devils (15th century) see *Jiggy's Magic Balls* in the Jiggy's Genes series (coming soon – Ed).

'What happened to that pen of yours anyway?' Pete asked. 'I kinda lost track of it.'

'I buried it in the garden.'

'The garden? Your garden?'

'Yeah. Till then, I kept putting it inside things or under things or on top of things, but it always came back to me after a while, to my hand, made me write or draw with it, and suddenly I was in the altogether. Then I remembered what Superman does with Kryptonite to stop it making him go weak or bad or whatever. He puts it inside something made of lead. My mum had an old lead box that used to belong to her gran, and I put the pen in it and buried it under the rockery. Did the trick. Never seen it since. The pen, that is.'

'Doesn't your mum ever wonder where her things keep vanishing to?' Angie asked.

'Only for a minute. Then another batch of ancient brain cells keel over and she goes and does some ironing.'

Suddenly Pete cleared his throat. Nervously. 'Um…people…'

He was pointing at the forest scene on the little stage. At first we wondered what he meant. Then we saw it. A hand sticking out of a painted bush.

'A prop,' Angie said.

'Looks so real,' I said.

'A good prop would. If it was real it'd be moving.'

'Not if it belonged to a dead person. Some famous actor Mooney the Loony walled up for revenge before catching a plane to Honolulu and a new identity.'

Angie went to the stage and climbed up on it. Leant over the hand, which was about as high as her knee.

'Looks even more real up close.'

Pete and I went to the stage, but didn't climb onto it.

'Touch it,' Pete said.

She reached out, and was about to touch it when its fingers twitched. She squealed, jumped back, fell off the stage. She would have fallen into our waiting arms, but our waiting arms had just dashed off to a respectable distance with the rest of us.

'It's real!' she squealed, scrambling to her feet – 'It's alive! Yrrrgh! Yrrrgh! Yrrrgh!' – and scurried to our respectable distance, where Pete was standing with his hands on his cheeks and I was dancing quietly, like I do when I see live human hands sticking out of bits of painted bush.

'What're we gonna do?' Pete wondered, once our nerves had settled a little and I'd stopped jigging about.

'Have to call the police,' said Angie.

'And spend the next three days and nights trying to explain why we broke in to a private barge without the owner's permission?' I said.

'Jig's right,' said Pete. 'Let's go.'

'We can't leave a live person bricked up in a wall!' Angie cried.

'Why not? No one'll know we were here if we don't tell them.'

'But he could die in there!'

'We could send the cops an anonymous text,' I suggested.

Angie went back to the stage and stared at the hand. 'No. We have to try and get him out.'

'You'd need a pickaxe to break through the wall,' I said. 'I could go home and see if we've got one...'

'Hang on, I don't think it is a wall. Look at that.'

She was pointing to a handle near the top of the forest.

'Pull it,' said Pete, still sharing my respectable distance.

Angie climbed back on the stage, reached up, gripped the handle. She pulled it, very cautiously, ready to jump back if the panel looked like falling on top of her. But it didn't fall, it came down easily, and as slowly as she needed it to. And then it was flat on the stage, and we realised six things, one after the other.

1. That the forest scene had been painted on the underside of a bed.

2. That the bed was one of those that can be pushed up out of the way when not in use.

3. That the hand belonged to the man who was in the bed.

4. That the man in the bed wasn't a man but a woman in an 'I Love Broadway' nightie.

5. That the woman in the 'I Love Broadway' nightie had been squashed between the mattress and the wall, upside down, with one hand sticking out the side.

6. That the woman in the 'I Love Broadway' nightie was Ms Mooney.

While the three of us swooned in shock,

107

Ms Mooney did not sit up, stretch her arms, and leap out of bed with a grateful 'Thank you so much for releasing me, here's a whopping great reward!' She didn't do these things because her eyes were closed.

Pete and I joined Angie in front of the stage and bed.

'Looks like she's copped it,' said Pete.

'She can't have,' said Angie. 'Her hand twitched.'

'Maybe it was her dying twitch.'

'Feel her garrotted artery,' I said to Angie. 'It's in the neck somewhere.'

She bent over Ms Mooney, felt around her neck while looking away and pulling a face.

'Feel anything?'

'Yeah, nauseous.'

'I mean in her neck.'

'Think so. Pulse of some sort.'

'Could be the one in your finger ends.'

'No, I'm sure it's in the neck.'

'Is there a heartbeat?'

'How would I know?'

'Feel for one.'

'You feel for one.'

'I don't think so.'

'Oh, you boys. Such wimps!'

She grabbed my wrist, jerked me half onto the stage, and slapped my palm on Ms Mooney's chest. She held it there while I scrambled to my knees beside the bed. Only when I was kneeling did she let go of my wrist, leaving my hand on the chest.

'Anything?' Angie asked.

'Not sure. Not used to feeling for teachers' heartbeats, specially in their chests.'

'Feel around a little.'

I looked at her. 'You're kidding, right?'

'No, it's the only way you'll find it, if there is one.'

I wasn't happy about this, but I knew it had to be done. I felt around for the heartbeat. I was still trying to track it down when something unexpected happened. The something unexpected was the opening of Ms Mooney's eyes. And what was the first thing those eyes saw?

Me.

And the second thing?

My hand on her bosom.

'*What are you doing?!*' she shrieked.

'Er, well…'

But she didn't wait for my carefully worded explanation. Her eyes turned black in a trice, and when they did that I got to my feet, kicked off my trainers, released my belt, dropped my jeans and pants, stepped out of them, and started to dance. Yes, dance. And this wasn't a Jiggy-type nervous dance. It was the dance of a marionette whose strings are being pulled by someone else. Someone powerful.

Pete and Ange didn't move for a minute. They just stood there, watching. Angie seemed a touch more fascinated than Pete, probably because a certain part of me was bouncing and flapping in all directions at once, which wasn't something she saw every day. She did manage to say 'Jig, try and stop,' but I couldn't. I jitterbugged across the little stage, arms in the air, naked from the waist down, wishing (because I wasn't doing this before an all-male audience) that I was only five years old instead of—

''Ello, 'ello, 'ello!'

Yes, folks, policemen still say that. I know this because I heard it first-hand, from the mouth of the one who was suddenly leaning in the window we'd entered by. I ran out of bounce quite soon after that and jumped into my clothes el swifto. Then I glanced at Ms Mooney. Her eyes were closed once more.

CHAPTER TWELVE

It was the man on the boat along the canal who'd called the cops. Some kids acting suspiciously, he'd told them. We were strong-armed off the barge and up the steps and shoved into a van with bars on the back window and driven at breakneck speed to the rozzer shop, where our explanation that we'd gone there to look for our missing teacher fell on cloth ears. (They might *just* have believed us if the first cop on the scene hadn't noticed me waving my todger about while dancing around that teacher's bed, with her still in it.) We got a heavy lecture while waiting for the Golden Oldies to screech to a halt outside, then the GOs drove us home while earbashing us with horrified statements ending in exclamation marks.

Back on the estate, P and A went to their house with her mum and his dad and I went to mine with mine. 'OK,' Dad said once we were indoors. 'At a stretch I can accept sneaking onto a teacher's boat to see if she's all right, but stripping off and doing the sabre dance because she *looked* at you? Come *on*, Jig!'

Mum said she hoped I was chucked out of the school play for this. I said that that wasn't likely because being chucked would be doing me a favour, and Ms Mooney wasn't big on favours for kids called McCue.

Ms Mooney. We learnt later that she'd been trapped upside down in the bed for two nights and most of a day. The bed had a powerful spring to make it easy to push up when it wasn't wanted, but as well as powerful the spring was sensitive. Too sensitive. Miss must have been in bed and turned over suddenly (or angrily, knowing her) and the spring had flipped the bed up and made a Mooney sandwich of her. As there was no way she could get out or force the bed down from the inside we'd probably saved her life, because they gave her oxygen on the way to the hospital and kept her in for observation for three whole days. They also had to fix her wrist. She'd got it trapped when the bed went up. Lucky the circulation wasn't cut off, they said.

As well as the knitted eyebrows of the police and stern warnings about entering private property and 'playing the fool' like they thought I'd been doing, we also got Serious Words from Mother Hubbard at school, but he seemed to believe most of our story eventually. Even he had trouble getting past my cabaret act, though, so he pretended that it hadn't occurred and changed the subject.

'We ought to go and see her,' Angie said as we were leaving school the day after they took Mooney to hospital.

'I've seen all I want of her,' I said. 'Specially in a nightie.'

'No, we should. I know you're not flavour of her year, but she's bound to be grateful to us now that she's fully conscious.'

'Don't count on it.'

'I want to go,' said Pete.

'You do?' I said in surprise.

'Sure, why not? She's always been OK with me.'

'Creep.'

'Come on, Jig,' said Angie. 'One for all and all for lunch?'

'Oh, you say that when it suits you. But when I say it, what do you do? You walk away.'

'That was different.'

'Well so's this.'

'Don't argue. You're coming.'

When we reached the hospital we whirled round in the revolving doors for a while, then tottered to the front desk with spinning heads. There was no one at the desk, but there was a little notice on it.

PLEASE RING THE BELL AND WAIT.

THANK YOU FOR YOUR PATIENTS.

'I see no bell,' I said.

'There was one last time we were here,' said Angie.

'Some sod pinched it,' said a disembodied voice.

Disembodied voices are always a bit worrying, so it's not really surprising that our three hearts went KERWHOOP and our six heels lifted off the ground in unison at the sound of that one. The disembodiment was solved, however, when a head popped up behind the desk. The head was also disembodied for a sec, but then the body it was attached to rose under it to about human height.

The bit of body between the head and the belt wore the blue shirt of Front Desk Man.

'You got a bed down there or something?' Pete asked him.

'No, I dropped me magazine. I have this hand tremble, see.'

He held up his hand. It was trembling. So was the nudist magazine it was holding.

'We're here to see Ms Mooney,' said Angie.

'What department?'

'Drama.'

'We don't have a Drama department.'

'No, that's at school. She's one of our teachers.'

'Well what's she doing here?'

'She's a patient.'

'Oh, a *patient*. Why didn't you say so?'

'I thought I did.'

'Which ward?'

'I don't know. She's under observation.'

'She should be,' I muttered.

The man seated himself on a little chair and typed something on his keyboard. 'Mooley, did you say?'

'Mooney, with an "n".'

'Ophelia Mooney?'

'That's her.'

'Orthopaedics, Ward 7.'

'Where's that?'

'Third floor. Lifts are over there, stairs right ahead of you. Ask someone at the nurses' station to show you to her.'

'Nurses have their own station?' said Pete. 'Own train too?'

Angie gripped him by the arm and marched him towards the stairs. When he resisted because he wanted to take the lift, she said that we were going by stair because stairs are healthier.

'I'm healthier than anyone in here,' Pete said.

'You won't be for long if you keep taking lifts.'

'I don't like hospitals,' I said as we started up.

Angie sighed. 'We know, you're always saying.'

'I'm not always saying. When have I said it before?'

'Last time we came here and the time before that, so don't say it again.'

'I won't. But I really don't like hospitals. Specially when I'm visiting enemies, which is all I seem to do.'*

---

* To read about a couple of those visits see *Ryan's Brain*.

We found the right ward because there were big arrows pointing to it, like that was where the treasure was buried. Before we pushed our way through the double doors I popped my mother's sunglasses on. I wasn't taking any more chances with Mooney.

'You can't wear sunglasses in a hospital,' said Angie.

'I see no sign,' I said. 'In fact I see nothing. These are really dark indoors.'

To prove it I crashed into a tea trolley. At least, I think it was a tea trolley. Might have been a bunch of kneeling nurses holding cups and saucers in the air and rattling them. Angie led me through the doors. 'He's blind,' she said to someone we almost collided with on the other side.

'He's stupid,' said Pete.

There were three nurses on duty at the nurses' station (no trains). Angie told them that we'd come to see Ophelia Mooney. One of the nurses said she'd just been moved to Bay 4, which was one of the two rooms across from the desk. Told us to go in without even frisking us for weapons.

There were five beds in the bay and Ms Mooney

was in one of them. I could tell this even with my mum's sunglasses on because it was lighter there than the corridor and her bed was by a window. She looked so different to the Mooney we were used to seeing. Her eyes were closed again and her mad hair was flatter than usual, and she looked...well, quite vulnerable, specially with one wrist and hand in plaster and a sling.

'OK, we've seen her,' I whispered. 'Can we go now?'

But Angie approached the bed. So did Pete. I stayed by the door. They were standing at her bedside for about fifteen seconds before Mooney's eyes opened. She started when she saw two teenage kids standing over her, but then she recognised them and...smiled. Yes, Ms Mooney smiled, and not in a mean, watch-what-you-say-to-me sort of way. Then the three of them were talking. I couldn't hear what they were saying but things seemed to be going pretty well, so I cranked up a sympathetic grin and aimed myself at the bedside. Ms Mooney turned her head as I drew near.

'Hi, Miss,' I said gaily.

When she saw who I was, the mouth that had been crowded with teeth a moment before became a tooth-free line. The fingers sticking out of the plastered hand stiffened, the unplastered hand became a claw, and her eyes shrank to the size of rabbit droppings.

'What do you want here?' she snapped.

'I'm visiting,' I said. 'To see how you are.'

'Don't give me that. What are you after?'

'After? Nothing, I...'

I glanced at Angie for help.

'He's with us,' she said.

Miss ignored her.

'What were you doing in my home?' she demanded – of me, just me, like I'd been the only one on the barge.

'Well, I...*we*...were worried about you. Wanted to see if—'

'Worried about me? You broke in and molested me while I was asleep!'

'Miss, I was feeling for a heartbeat.'

'Feeling for a heartbeat! Others might fall for that, not me.'

The four people in the other beds were all

looking our way now.

'Ange,' I whispered, trying to quieten things down a bit. 'Tell her.'

'It's true, Miss, he was,' she said.

She might have been invisible and gagged for all the notice Mooney took of her.

'Take those glasses off!'

My hand flew to my glasses. Held them firmly in place.

'Can't. Eye condition. Told you before.'

'Eye condition! Do you take me for a fool? Off with them!'

'What, so you can make me do something to get me in trouble again?'

'If you don't take them off, I'll scream.'

That was it. I'd had enough.

'So scream.'

And she opened her mouth and…screamed.

We left in a hurry. Just before the security guards arrived to toss us out the window.

CHAPTER THIRTEEN

That hospital visit really brought me down, I don't know why. Yes, I do. I hadn't done anything wrong, but people (not just Mooney) still had suspicions that I'd been up to something on the barge. Even Mum and Dad kept giving me these odd looks, like they were thinking 'What kind of monster have we not been reading bedtime stories to all these years?'

I was still a bit broody on Monday. Pete and Angie tried to jolly me along, but it didn't help much. What helped a *little* was hearing that Ms Mooney wouldn't be back in school for a few days and that Mrs Gamble would be taking the after-school rehearsals till then, plus Wednesday's Drama class. By Tuesday I was almost back to normal: daydreaming out of the window in this class or that and trying to cheer up downtrodden teachers with lively banter. I even quite enjoyed one class. It was with this supply teacher, Mr

Bakelite, who'd taken us for Food Technology a few times in a previous term.* Cookery hadn't seemed to be Mr B's first love, but he was really into his latest subject. I've no idea what the lesson was *supposed* to be, but the stuff he wanted to tell us about made his eyes light up and his little ginger moustache quiver.

'There's a wealth of stories about gods and heroes in ancient times,' he began. 'Greek myths in particular fascinate us.'

'Speak for yourself,' said Ryan.

'In Greek mythology, the gods were born out of the dark void of empty space, which they called Chaos—'

'Like some of our lessons,' muttered Nafeesa Aslam.

'—and the father of them all, Uranus—'

'No need to be rude, sir!' shouted Harry Potter, the twonk.

'—sired many children, but he thought them ugly and locked them away, out of sight. This didn't please his wife, who encouraged one of their sons, Cronos, to overthrow Uranus and – you'll like this bit – cut off his dad's privates.' (Whoops

---

* Along with Jiggy's previous hospital visits, the most disastrous of Mr Bakelite's lessons is described in *Ryan's Brain*.

of approval from the girls and a smattering of 'Oooohs', mostly from boys.) 'Thus Cronos became king of the gods.'

'Better than king of the bleedin' fairies,' said Pitwell, lobbing a borrowed pencil sharpener at Pete. Pete ducked and it hit me. I caught the sharpener as it bounced off my nose and lobbed it back at Pitwell. It missed him and hit Marlene Bronson in the next row. She didn't catch it and pass it on. She jumped up and threatened to come and sort me out, and she might have too – Bronson's favourite pastime is boy bashing – if Mr Bakelite hadn't ordered us all to settle down, settle down, and stay in our seats please. When we were quiet enough for him to hear himself speak again, he went on.

'Upon becoming king, Cronos married his sister, Rhea, but when—'

'Married his *sister*? That's disgusting!' said Holly Gilder.

'—when she bore him children, Cronos, worried by a prophesy that he, like his father, would be overthrown by one of them, ate them one after the other as soon as they were born.'

'Not a vegetarian then?' I said.

'Now as you can imagine, Rhea wasn't overjoyed about her husband's behaviour, so when her sixth child, Zeus, was born she wrapped up a large stone and handed it to Cronos, telling him it was the boy.'

'And he swallowed that?' Gemma Kausa asked dubiously.

'Both the story and the stone, yes, seems so.'

'One stoned god, eh?' said Milo Dakin.

'I've heard of Zeus!' Trevor Fisher said, like he'd just found a gold bar under his desk.

'Everyone's heard of Zeus, Fish,' I said wearily.

'I ent,' said Eejit Atkins.

Mr Bakelite spread his hands and lowered them slowly like he was pressing the noise down. When we were quiet he said, 'Zeus was raised in secret away from home, and when he became a young man he defeated his father in battle and sent him into exile. That's one version anyway. There are so many interpretations of these tales that you may well hear or read a different version from another source.'

'None of this is true, is it?' said Julia Frame. She sounded worried in case it was.

'Myths are colourful stories passed down through

125

the generations and embellished along the way, Julia. Just that. Stories.'

'Tell us about some of the old heroes, sir,' Nirmal Sandhu said.

'You mean the ones with fighting and killing,' sneered Jodie Gold.

Nirmal beamed. 'Yeah!'

'And the monsters,' said Ubik Sprinz. 'Tell us about the monsters.'

Several girls groaned.

Mr Bakelite smiled. 'Heroes and monsters, eh? There are plenty of both in Greek mythology. Among the Greek heroes there was Heracles – Hercules, if you prefer – and Jason (of Argonaut fame), and Odysseus, and Perseus, and—'

'Can't you just pick one and bang on about him for a minute and a half till the boys get bored, sir?' Angie suggested.

Mr B nodded. 'OK, let's give Perseus a spin. Anyone know his story?'

'I used to,' chirped Milo Dakin. 'My dad gave me this big book about ancient heroes and stuff when I was eight. Might have been nine. I remember something about Perseus, but I've forgotten what.'

'Well let me refresh your memory. Perseus is famous for many things, but his most renowned deed was the slaying of Medusa, most fearsome of all the gorgons. Anyone know what a gorgon was?'

'A woman that turned people to stone?' Fiala Kolinski asked.

'Not a woman, Fiala, though she was indeed female. Most versions of the story have her as a vile creature with writhing snakes for hair, whose very gaze turned to stone anyone who met her eye.'

'Sounds like Ms Mooney,' I said. No one laughed.

'Knowing that he mustn't look directly upon her,' Mr Bakelite went on, 'Perseus devised a cunning plan. Fiala?'

'Er…something to do with a mirror?'

'Not quite. You might be thinking of the basilisk, a small serpent that could kill with a look. One of the ways to destroy a basilisk was to hold a mirror to it. It would expire on seeing its own reflection.'

'What about this Mormon?' Wapshott asked.

'Gorgon,' said Mr Bakelite. 'Perseus, keen to despatch Medusa, who'd been running rather amok of late, called on three of her sisters, who were very

127

old. (In fact, they were born old.) These sisters had just one eye between them, which they passed around among themselves to take turns to see the world. While they were passing the eye, Perseus snatched it and said he wouldn't return it until they told him where to find Medusa. He can't have been a very honourable bloke because once they'd directed him to her he threw the eye in a lake.'

'Smart hero!' said Toklas in a dungeon-deep American film trailer voice.

'Did he get Medusa?' Kelly Ironmonger asked.

'Indeed he did,' Mr Bakelite said. 'When he reached her cave, Perseus slyly crept up on her, avoiding looking directly at her by viewing her reflection in his shield, which was made of highly polished bronze, and...' – he grinned around – '...sliced off her head.'

'Cool,' said Eejit Atkins.

'There's a lot more to that story, and indeed, the legend of Perseus, but those are the bare details. If you would like more information on him and—'

'Tell us about some other heroes!' one of the boys shouted.

Mr Bakelite paused. He looked surprised. He

didn't usually get this much enthusiasm in his lessons.

'I could talk about deeds of mythological derring-do all day, but I think we have to try and please the ladies as well as you bloodthirsty boys. How about a spot of romance now...?'

This attempt to win favour with the girls backfired badly. Amid indignant protests from several of them, Angie jumped to her feet.

'Sir, that is so *sexist*! And so out of date! Girls today do *not* want all that soppy, lovey-dovey stuff!'

'I do,' said one of them.

'Shut up, Julia,' said Angie.

The rest of the lesson did not go well. For Mr Bakelite anyway. Fun for us kids, though.

CHAPTER FOURTEEN

As the weather was so nice that Wednesday, Mrs Gamble took us actors to the playing field for the afternoon Drama period. The non-actors had to go to the craft room and carry on working on the scenery and costumes. Some of them weren't so over the moon about that, specially when we walked off laughing and bowing like real luvvies.

There's a corner of the playing field that's not used for games because it's got trees in it. This is known as Smokers Wood (guess why), though it's not only smokers who go there on the sly. You know this because some days there are quite a few things amid the trees that you don't want too many eyefuls of. But the day before our session all the grass had been cut and the woody bit had been cleared out, so we could sit down without checking too hard what we were about to park ourselves on. I was annoyed, though. As it was a warm day we'd been allowed to leave our jackets up in the craft room, and I'd forgotten to take my mum's sunglasses out of my pocket, and I needed them because it was so bright. Angie had her silver wraparounds with her, but she wouldn't lend them to me.

'But you're not wearing them,' I said.

'I might when we start rehearsing,' she answered.

'So lend them to me till then.'

'No. I might put them on any minute.'

And she flounced on ahead. Women. So selfish.

A few of the props were finished and we took them down with us. One was the ass's head, which looked more like a long-eared camel to me. When I tried it on it smelt of glue, and the eyes were too high, so I had to keep my head down to see out.

'Suits you, McCue!' the distant voice of Ryan shouted.

I lifted the head off mine. 'If you wore it, Fairy Pissbunny, no one'd know the difference!'

The idea today was for us to try and get through our lines without eyeing the script. Pete and a few of the others who'd done more private rehearsing than was healthy made it most of the way through, but it was a struggle for the rest of us. We had a prompter today, though – Julia Frame, who'd moaned so much about not being in the production that Mrs G had given her the job. This cheered Julia up a little if not hugely. 'It's not a *part*,' she whined, 'but at least I feel part *of* it now.'

'Swap with me if you like,' I offered kindly.

She looked at Mrs Gamble. 'Miss?'

Who smiled. 'I'm only standing in for Ms Mooney till she rejoins us. I can't change the casting, and she must have chosen Jiggy for a reason.'

'She did,' I said. 'To see me make a complete crotch of myself in public.'

Because Mrs G didn't snap or shout if we got words wrong, like Mooney did, some of us who'd been dragged screaming into the play were almost enjoying it now. Even I wasn't quite as anti as I had been. Just wished my latest archenemy wasn't taking charge again tomorrow.

I soon discovered that it was pretty hot as well as smelly inside my head. The ass's, I mean. Also, when I had it on I had to shout to be heard. We were coming to the end of one of my scenes, and I was jumping around a bit to liven things up when everyone started laughing and pointing at me.

'What's up?' I yelled through the ass's mouth.

'Never mind,' Mrs Gamble said. 'Finish the scene, everyone.'

When we finished it and I took the head off I saw that one of the ass's ears had come away and was hanging down like a big earring.

'Obviously not made in China,' I said, flicking the ear.

'Jiggy,' Mrs G said. 'You won't have anything to say for the rest of the session, so why not take the head up to the craft room and ask someone to reglue that ear?'

'I'd rather stay, Miss. Nicer out here.'

She shook her head. 'Time's running out. The ear needs fixing. Go on, there's a good old Bottom.'

'And I thought you were fun,' I grouched.

'Me?' she said. 'You're confusing me with someone else. Go.'

I sighed, but tucked the big head that looked like a camel under my arm (that looked like an arm) and was about to go when I remembered how bright it was away from the trees. I looked for Angie. Maybe she'd lend me her glasses now. She was chatting to a couple of others about their next scene and had left her silver wraparounds on her bag by one of the trees. I sidled across, scooped them up, dropped them in the upturned ass's head. I could always put them somewhere she would come across them later, and there were plenty of people she could accuse of nicking them till then.

'And don't go larking about and putting that head on in school please!' Mrs Gamble called as I started away.

'Me, Miss? Would I?'

'Indeed you would. It's common knowledge that Jiggy McCue never passes up a chance for a jape.'

'Miss, I need a slash!' (Eejit Atkins.)

Mrs G turned to him. 'Ralph, *do* phrase it differently.'

This was quite a poser for Atkins, but he tried. 'Erm…slash Miss need I?'

She shook her head in a what-am-I-going-to-do-with-you sort of way. 'Very well, go with Jiggy. Come straight back when you're done.'

'Atkins doesn't need me with him to take a pee, Miss.'

'No, I'm sure he doesn't, but as you're going that way…?'

'I'm going to the artsy-fartsy room. No bogs there.'

'But there are some nearby. Go that far together. We're not supposed to let pupils roam the school in packs while lessons are in progress.'

'You need more than two for a pack. Anyone else wanna come?'

Hands shot up.

'Jiggy, go. And Ralph. Now where were we?' she said to the others.

I marched on. Atkins had to run to catch up.

'Jig,' he said when he made it. 'Kin I try the 'ead?'

I fished Angie's shades out and put them on. 'No.'

'Aw, go on, I never wore no donkey's 'ead before.'

'Get away, you're wearing one now.'

'No. I'm not. This is me own.'

'Mrs G said we weren't to wear it.'

'She din't. She said you wuzn't t' wear it, not me.'

This was true. And if he wore it I wouldn't have to carry it. I glanced back. Miss and the others were too busy with the next scene to bother about us. I looked at the buildings ahead. No bored teachers standing at the windows while their

135

classes slaved quietly behind them.

'OK. But mess around in my head and it's the knacker's yard for you.'

We stopped walking while he put his head inside the ass's. I heard his distant muffled voice.

'What?' I said.

He lifted the head. 'I can't see.'

'Look through the eye-holes. They're the two bits with light shining through.'

He lowered the head again and tilted it this way and that and up and down. His muffled voice again.

'Now what?' I said.

He lifted the head. 'Got 'em.'

'And if you really have to speak, you've got to project your voice.'

'Do what?'

'Speak up.'

'OH!' he shouted.

'When you've got the head on.'

'Oh.'

He dropped the head back in place and we started walking again.

'JIG!'

'What now?'

'KIN YOU 'EAR ME?'

I picked up the ear that needed fixing and shouted into it. 'NO! NOW SHUT THAT ASS'S HOLE AND GIVE ME SOME PEACE!'

At the top of the playing field, I pushed open the double doors and we entered the first of the many corridors between us and the craft room. Eejit kept the head on and I kept Angie's glasses on.*

It was so quiet indoors, even though the building was stuffed with people. A spooky sort of quiet, like a church, only without the pews, Bibles, stained glass, begging bowl and religion. Being in school and out of class when lessons are going on all around me makes me a bit jumpy, if you want to know. Mr Hubbard too, I reckon, going by the way he opened his door and leapt in the air as we strolled by. Maybe it was the sight of his double reflection in Angie's sunglasses, or maybe it was Eejit in the ass's head, I didn't ask.

'Are you trying to give me a heart attack?' he demanded as he came down from the ceiling.

'Not me,' I said. 'Can't speak for Atkins.'

'That's Atkins in there?'

'Yes.'

---

* They weren't as dark to look out of as my mother's, plus a glimpse of myself in the glass doors had shown that I looked kind of cool in them.

'Why?'

'Cos he's a moron, sir.'

'Why are you wearing sunglasses indoors?'

'I get these headaches.'

'Ah. And you're not in a lesson because...?'

'Atkins is going for a pee and I'm on my way to the craft room.'

'Oh, the craft room. I was going there myself. Look, save me a trip and give Ms Mooney a message for me, will you?'

'Ms Mooney's not in till tomorrow, sir.'

'Officially no, but she came in a little while ago. Wanted to see how the prop-making was coming along.'

'Oh, no,' I said.

'What's wrong?'

'Ms Mooney, that's what's wrong.' It was out before I could stop it.

'What do you mean?'

Well, in for a penny. 'She hates me, sir.'

'Hates you? Jiggy, you've explained what happened on her boat. It's all cleared up. And teachers don't hate their pupils.'

'Some of them do. She does. She's got a real

downer on me. Always making me do unnatural things.'

'Un… What sort of things?'

'Things I don't want to do.'

'Yes, well,' he said. 'This is a school, y'know.'

'Yeah, I know, but—'

'And at school we can't always do what we would prefer to do. We're here to learn.'

'Oh, I'm learning all right. I'm learning not to be in the same room as Ms Mooney if I can help it.'

He came over all stern at this. 'Enough. Go to the craft room and do what you're told to do, and let's have an end to this nonsense.'

I realised my mistake. Never trash one teacher to another, even a head one. They stick together. It's them against us, and the odds are in their favour. As long as we're in school we lose. Fact of life.

Mother went back into his office, forgetting that he was going to give me a message for Ms Mooney. Fine. I didn't want to give her *anything*, even a message from someone else.

CHAPTER FIFTEEN

Knowing that Mooney was in the craft room made me even less eager to get there, so to waste a bit of time I went into the Boys with Atkins. He was still wearing the ass's head as he trotted to the urinal and unzipped. I admired the latest graffiti while I waited. After a minute he yelled through the big fat camelish trap.

'Jig! The eyes is too 'igh! I can't see daan!'

'So what do you want me to do about it?'

''Old it fer me, will ya?!'

'Hold the head?'

'Nah, me joint!'

'Eejit, are you insane? Just aim. Hope for the best.'

Pause. Sound of splashing water.

'I done it!'

'Congratulations. Medal's in the post.'

He zipped up, screamed in a muffled sort of way, and doubled over to nurse the loose bit he'd trapped. When he'd got over it enough to limp to the door, I barred the way.

'Wash your stinking hands, Atkins.'

'Woffor?'

'Because you've probably peed all over them, that's woffor.'

'Yeah, but they're dry nah.'

'Eejit,' I said. 'Those hands are not touching my ass until they've been washed.'

I had to turn the taps on and off for him because he couldn't see them with the ass's eyes so high on the head. Then I had to steer him to the roller towel and help him dry his hands.

When we were finally outside he said something I didn't catch. I leant closer. He gripped the top and bottom lips of the head and shouted: 'I'll see ya later!'

I leant back, little-fingering my deafened ear. 'OK, gimme the head and...' I paused. I'd had a thought. A way to get out of seeing Mooney. 'No, tell you what. Come to the craft room with me.'

'But Mrs G said—'

'I know what Mrs G said. Don't worry, I'll clear it with her when this is over.'

When we reached the door of the craft room, him still wearing the head, me still in Angie's silver sunglasses, I told him what I wanted him to do.

'You go in, tell Mooney the ass's head's ear's coming off and ask her to get it fixed. Repeat that.'

'I go in, tell 'er the 'ead's ear's come orf and she has to fix it.'

'No, not the *head's* ear, cretin. She'll think you mean Hubbard's and probably call an ambulance. The one you're wearing. On top of your own.'

'Why dun you do it?'

'Because it only needs one of us, and you're the one.'

I turned the door handle, shoved him inside, and pulled the door to, leaving just enough gap to see what occurred. The craft room was as silent as the corridors, even though work was being done in there. Ms Mooney wasn't keen on chatter unless it was in a script. A lot of the kids were bent over the costumes and props. Others were putting finishing touches to the forest.

'Bottom! Hm! Fooling about as ever, I see!'

Mooney's voice. I craned to peer through a different angle of the crack. She was glaring at Eejit in the ass's head. When he held up the loose ear like he was trying to hear what she said, she gripped him by a shoulder and marched him back to the door. I got set to run, but she didn't come out. She spoke quietly to him just the other side of the door, so the class couldn't hear. But I could, in the corridor.

'I was hoping to bump into you,' she said to Atkins. 'You seem to have convinced everyone that you came to my home to see if I was all right. But I know differently. I know that if you hadn't been interrupted you would have abused me while I was helpless. The papers are full of miscreants like you, and most of them get away with it. Well you will *not*, young man!'

Well, well, she thought it was *me* she was talking to. All right, so Atkins was wearing the ass's head and she couldn't see his face, but he's much shorter than me. Even though the head gave him a spot of extra height, you'd think she'd have realised that if it was me inside it I'd be looking down at her even more than usual, not right at her like he was. I heard Eejit's muffled voice inside the head, but Mooney wasn't having any excuses or

143

arguments that she thought were coming from me. I saw her eyes narrow, and knew they were darkening. Any second she would make Eejit do whatever she had in mind for me. The poor little peanut wouldn't know what hit him.

I pushed the door back. It hit Ms Mooney on the shoulder.

'You've got the wrong Bottom,' I said as she jumped back.

Her black eyes widened. 'But…' she said.

'Exactly,' I replied.

Then they narrowed again, and became blacker still. 'So. Another of your sorry attempts at humour at my expense.'

'No, I wasn't trying to pull anything. Mrs Gamble sent us to—'

She held up her hand. 'I don't want to hear it.' She turned to Eejit. 'You. Take that head off.'

Eejit lifted the head. When she saw who it was she told him to put the head 'over there' and that she would deal with him in a minute. Most of the kids in the room were looking our way now. 'Get back to work!' she said sharply. Some of them went on looking. 'All of you!' she shouted. The rest looked away. That was when I decided that I wasn't going to be bullied any more by this woman, even if she was a teacher.

'You don't like anyone much, do you?' I said.

'I get on with those whom I need to,' she said. 'But every so often someone comes along and rubs me up the wrong way—'

'That must be painful.'

'—by making smart-aleck remarks like that, and then I just *know* we're not going to be best pals.'

'Oh yes, then what? You make them do things in public to embarrass them or get them in trouble or hurt them?'

Her eyes became black dots. 'Or get them suspended.'

'Suspended? Me, you mean?'

'I think you have it coming.'

'Get me suspended and I won't be able to make a fool of myself in your stupid play.'

She smiled coldly. 'I'm sure the one will be adequate compensation for the other. Remove those glasses please.'

'No chance.'

She reached out to snatch them off my face, but

145

I stepped back and she missed. This made her madder than ever. Through Angie's shades her eyes actually seemed to glow, and her hair, her mad, sticky-up hair, seemed to move. I know these things were optical illusions, but the glowing eyes and crazy hair cartwheeled my mind back to the last time I'd imagined such effects: the day before, in Mr Bakelite's class. He'd been talking about this mythical female-type monster with snakes for hair who turned people to stone if they looked at her, and I'd joked that she sounded like Ms Mooney. He'd mentioned something else too. Something about mirrors…

'I *said*,' Miss Mooney snarled, 'remove them!'

I was about to say something like 'On your broomstick, Miss' when a movement behind her caught my eye. Atkins, waving his arms to attract my attention. He held a sword that had been made for the play and was making swiping motions at the back of Mooney's neck. I was very tempted to give him the nod, but I suddenly remembered the thing Mr Bakelite had said about mirrors, and I thought, 'I wonder…' and made this big decision to give it a shot. If I was wrong and she made me do the thing she had in her warped little mind, I'd probably get suspended like she intended, but if it worked...

I raised Angie's glasses and lodged the frames on the top of my head, like poseurs and rich wallies the world over.

'This do?' I said.

'It will,' said she.

Then she leant very close, and her eyes went totally dark, and I immediately felt myself being drawn into them. The point of no return was nigh. Another six heartbeats and I'd be doing whatever terrible thing it pleased her to make me do, just like before. But there was a difference this time. The difference was that one smidgen of my mind was ready for her, and that tiny part was enough to order my head to flick upward ever so slightly and drop Angie's sunglasses over my eyes again. And when my eyes were covered...

Mooney's hold on me was instantly broken!

But there was something else too. Something even better. The eyes she was now looking into were her own, reflected in those mirror-like lenses, and, just as I'd hoped, the full charge of what she'd aimed at me bounced right back at her.

She opened her mouth. Began to shout.

I won't write down what she shouted, but it must have been everything she'd meant me to say, and this time it *definitely* wasn't Shakespearean. It was the sort of language no kid can get away with in school without getting a suspension at *least*. And she couldn't stop herself. She tried – almost tied herself in knots trying to get her gob to clam – but nothing worked, and that made her madder than ever. Now her hair really was standing on end, and her eyes really were glowing – with uncontrollable rage, all of it aimed at me behind my protective silver lenses. As she couldn't get at me with her eyes, she cast about for something to attack me with, saw the sword in Eejit's hand, and ran at him. He covered his head, the worm, and she snatched the sword and spun round, all set to throw herself at me.

'Swift-exit time, McCue!'

That's what I might have said if I'd been a hero in a graphic novel. Even though I wasn't in a graphic novel I decided that it made sense to back speedily into the corridor and put the door between us, and that's what I did. The closed door didn't shut Mooney up though. She was still coming towards it from the other side, voice rising in a shrill shriek full of terrible words.

'Ah, Jiggy. Silly me, forgot to give you that message for Ms Mooney.'

I whirled. Mother Hubbard, waltzing along the corridor, all smiles.

He was almost at the door when he heard the shouting in the craft room. His smile dipped.

'What's all that?'

And then I thought, 'Well, why not? Go for it, Jig, what's to lose?'

'It's Ms Mooney, sir. She's doing what I told you she does, only worse. Said she's gonna kill me, and all I did was go in the room. There are witnesses.'

He looked like he might panic at this. Like a situation was coming up that he wouldn't know how to handle without Miss Prince to stand behind.

'Jiggy, I'm sure you've misunderstood. I'm sure she—'

'No, sir. This is what she does. I told my mum, and she said that if Miss ever behaved like this again she'd go to the school governors and get her kicked out, and probably you too for employing her.'

I'd just said this when Mooney wrenched the door back and charged out waving the sword and screaming language that had never before been heard from a teacher at Ranting Lane. Not out loud anyway, not shouted. Mother Hubbard backed away in horror, tripped over his feet, and fell to the floor. Ms Mooney saw him go down, but she didn't stop shouting those words or help him up. She couldn't. That was one huge hex she'd aimed at me, and by the sound of it, it still had quite a way to run.

CHAPTER SIXTEEN

Ms Mooney disappeared after that. No more Drama with her, yippee. That Sunday, Angie suggested that we go and see if her barge was still on the canal. I said count me out, and this time I stuck to it, so she and Pete went on their own.

'Her barge is still there,' Pete said when they got back.

'Did you see her?'

'No, but some men were taking that bed out, so she's not stuck in it again.'

'Pity,' I said. 'This time we could have left her.'

'That's vindictive,' said Angie.

'I know. Don't care.'

With Mooney off the stage, Mrs G took over the play rehearsals. With her in charge it wasn't such a bad thing to be involved in, and I elbowed the idea of pulling a last-minute sickie. Well, I'd got this far, the person who made me do things I didn't want to was gone, and as Angie said, 'It's your big

chance to show off before an *invited* audience.'
Hard to resist, that.

As I got happier about being in the play, Julia Frame warmed to the idea of not being in it. She'd really taken to prompting, and as she had to do quite a lot of it she started to feel we couldn't manage without her. She was probably right. Eejit's moronic Puck didn't get much better, but at least it gave us a laugh, and Ryan came close to violence a few times about being called variations of Fairy Peaseblossom, but like me he stuck with it. Hegarty made the most of Titania too. Really camped her up. Mrs G didn't mind that. Mooney would have.

As for Pete, he got more and more impossible. It was Shakespeare, Shakespeare, Shakespeare, morning, noon and text message. His chat was stuffed with 'prithees', 'wherefores' and 'have-at-thee, varlets.' By the end he was downloading whole other plays by the Bod, memorising words, lines, entire speeches, and letting us know about it. Like one afternoon when everyone was shimmying out of the school gates, he said in a very loud voice, 'I wish you well and so I take my leave, I pray you know me when we meet again,' and someone swore at him, and he said, 'While thou livest keep a good tongue in thy head,' which would have got him a thumping if Angie hadn't jumped to his rescue.

The *Midsummer Night's* scenery looked pretty reasonable from a distance. So did the three trees that had been built, and the clumps of plywood grass designed to be dotted about the stage for us to trip over. There were a few cockups with the costumes – too tight, big, long, short, a sleeve or leg missing – but it all got sorted in time for the show. *Just* in time in a couple of cases. Then all that was left was for us actors to strut our stuff. Our stage was the one in the main hall where the teachers gather on Assembly mornings to scowl down at us kids like they're about to give us thirty years in solitary.

The hall was three-quarters full on the evening of our one and only performance. The audience was made up of parents, kids from school, and a smattering of teachers who hadn't been sharp enough to come up with excuses to get out of it. Most of the teachers came as they were, but some of the parents had smartened themselves up for the occasion. One, a single father I guessed, wore a black hat with the brim turned down, dark glasses, and an old-fashioned raincoat (also black) with loops on the shoulders. Looked like a Mafia hit man on his night off. Mrs Gamble, who'd remained backstage to stop us burning the school down, told us there was also a reporter and a snapper from the free local paper in the audience.

'They must be desperate, turning out for a half-term school play,' said Ryan.

'Probably couldn't believe their luck,' I said.

'What luck?'

'Chance to get pics of you dressed as a fairy.'

'At least they won't get any of me in a donkey's head,' he sneered.

'No. But if they print one of me in it, no one'll know it's me, will they, Fanny Piddleblossom?'

He lunged at me, I ducked, and he got Marlene Bronson in a necklock instead. Marlene kneed him in the prunes. Ryan spent the next ten minutes on the floor, cradling them.

Even if it was only the yokel press, them being there made some of us even more nervous than we were already. The thought of having to say those words and ponce about in wacky costumes in front of an audience had been bad enough, but knowing that thousands of unsuspecting householders might soon be gawping at us over their porridge…well, there was more than one last-minute dash to the bogatorium before the play kicked off.

Even Pete was nervous when the curtains were finally yanked back, but after a shaking fit when he first came on, he got a grip and soon everyone could see that he was the best thing in the play, including the scenery. He hardly made a wrong move and only fluffed twice, while some of us mangled line after line, glancing constantly at Julia for our next words. She was crouched down in front of the stage with the script, and all of us except Atkins tried to make out that we weren't looking for a prompt. Atkins came right out with it, no messing – 'Jools, wot's me next bit?' – which had the audience in fits.

As the play got going and we settled down, it got a bit less scary. It helped that the audience laughed in some of the right places. My mum and dad were among them, of course. I wished they'd brought Swoozie – I know she would've loved to see big bruv on stage – but they'd got a sitter in for her. Mum sat bolt upright all the way through, beaming almost nonstop, while Dad had his hands over his eyes most of the time. Angie's mum and Pete's dad were with them. Audrey Mint was sitting on the other side of my mother and also beaming a lot of the time. Oliver Garrett wasn't embarrassed like my dad. Whenever Pete came on, his jaw dropped. He couldn't believe that his jokey, war-game-loving son, who hated homework and most other school stuff, was the absolute star of a Shakespeare play.

Once we'd realised that we could do this, some of us followed Hegarty's lead (by halfway through his fairy queen was Widow Twankey's deranged mother) and began overacting big-time. I started ad-libbing when I forgot what came next, and so did some of the others. This led to a few pauses while those who were sticking to the script, like Pete, tried to steer the thing back on course, but it got us some extra chortles from the audience. At one point, while wearing the ass's head and prancing about unscriptedly, I thought how Ms Mooney would have murdered me for acting up like this. She would probably have sent the Mafia hit man in the audience to take me out, I thought, and lifted the ass's head to overact a hearty guffaw. The press photographer flashed. I glanced into the wings at Mrs Gamble. She raised her eyes to heaven, but laughed.

And then it was over. Steffany and Nafeesa, who were in charge of the curtains, pulled them across while the audience clapped. Mrs Gamble got us all to stand in a hasty line to take a bow. I hadn't been wearing the ass's head by the end of the play, but I tucked it under my arm and pushed my way between Pete and Hegarty at centre stage a second before Steff and Naffy hauled the curtains back. Then I dropped the ass's head over Hegarty's. Big round of laughs from the audience. I bowed. As I straightened up I noticed that the Mafia hit man had taken his dark glasses off and raised the brim of his hat. For the first time I could see his face properly. And when I saw it, I realised he wasn't a man at all.

He was Ms Mooney.

She'd obviously snuck in in disguise to see what a hash we made of the play without her. She'd witnessed all our larking about, fluffing, ad-libbing and the rest. What was that thought I'd had? That if she'd seen me horsing around in the ass's head she'd have sent the Mafia hit man to get me? Well, she hadn't needed to. She *was* the Mafia hit man.

The instant I realised this I also realised three other things.

1. Her eyes were locked on mine, and they were pitch-black and gleaming.

2. I hadn't got any sunglasses to protect me against her.

3. She was going to get her revenge, and this time there wasn't a thing I could do about it.

My costume was a jerkin sort of thing over loose-fitting trousers. No belt, so I didn't have one to undo. Or a zip to unzip. All I had to do as I turned my back on the audience was grip the material and tug south. 'McCue, you steaming heap, what're ya doing?' someone hissed.

'Pull 'em up, Jig, pull 'em up!' said Ange.

But I didn't pull 'em up. I couldn't. All I could do was waggle my bare cheeks at the audience, then waggle them some more. And more. When I heard this welling-up human sort of sound I groaned. Obvious what was happening. Everyone thought

I was mooning because that's what brain-dead teenage boys do to insult onlookers. Mr Hubbard, in the front row just below the stage with Miss Prince, was getting a bum's-eye view, and it was a view he wouldn't appreciate. It looked like Mooney was going to get me suspended after all.

But then...

'Good old Bottom!'

This was from someone in the audience. Not a kid either.

'Huh?' I said. Or maybe I just thought it.

I couldn't pull my pants up yet, but I managed to crank my neck round and look over my shoulder. I'd been half expecting the mob to be moving towards the stage to beat me to death with the huge tubs of popcorn they hadn't got. But they weren't moving towards me. Weren't even sweeping out of the hall in disgust. Nay, they were laughing. Then they started cheering, and whistling, and applauding all over again. Well, what do you know? They thought it was a hoot that the boy who'd played Bottom was showing his *actual* bottom at the final curtain!

I could tell from her expression that the

159

audience's amusement didn't please Ms Mooney. Approval was the last thing she'd expected. She jumped out of her seat, pushed past the others in her row, and stomped out of the hall in a fury. As she went I found that I could pull my trousers up. This I did, without much ado. When they were once again at their correct height I turned to face the audience and took another bow. A long, low one.

Well, that's it. End of story. This time Ms Mooney really did disappear. No one ever saw her again. Her or her barge. But I've never been able to shake the feeling that she's still out there somewhere and that one of these days I'll turn a corner and there she'll be, waiting to skewer me with her killer eyes and make me do something I'll never *ever* live down. That thought will probably keep my nerves jangling and me jigging until the day I crumble to dust and get swept under the carpet.

What a life.

Oh, by the way. There was a picture of our play in the local paper. Just one. Of me. My back view, naturally. And above it, in big bold type, were the words: BOTTOM OF THE CLASS.

I was the school hero for days afterwards.

With the kids anyway.

ntroducing an exciting brand-new series...

JiGGY'S GENES

...in which we meet a whole host of Jiggy's ancestors
and discover that, through centuries past,
there have *always* been Jiggys!

on't miss the first book,

JiGGY'S MAGIC BALLS

where we meet a 15th-century Jiggy...

Turn the page to read an extract!

CHAPTER ONE

As told by the 15th-century Jiggy...

Well, here I am, up to my goolies in mud and rust, talking to myself once again. I talk to myself because I'm the only one who listens to me. No one listens because I'm just another peasant kid. I'm not even a squire yet, even if I do serve a knight with a full suit of armour. My knight is Sir Bozo de Beurk, and his armour is rubbish. Sir Bozo isn't the brightest light in the knight sky, but at least his wife isn't about any more. His wife was called Ratface. Well, that's what I called her. Lady Ratface thought she was really something. Always trying to make out that her origins weren't almost as humble as mine. 'Ow! So-nace-to-mate-yer,' she'd coo when she was introduced to people she wanted to impress. Didn't impress me one bit. Not that she tried. Just shouted orders at me the whole time and called me names. I wasn't fond of her.

As well as a bad-tempered wife, Sir Bozo had

a castle that looked like its only ambition was to fall down. Crumbling old dump, breezy as a turnip-eater's bottom, but he was quite attached to it because it had been in his family for at least a generation and a half. When Lady Ratface decided she could do better than him in the knight department she hired this dodgy legal wizard Spivvel Merlin who had a rep for getting good settlements for greedy wives. Sir Bozo wasn't hugely rich, so all Merlin got for Lady R was the castle, which she immediately put up for sale. At first no one bought it – there was a recession on – but then Spiv Merlin himself made an offer for it, so it was his now, which really choked Sir B because he and Merlin had been mortal enemies since they were at school together.

After the divorce, the only possessions Sir Bozo was left with were his horse, a shed on boggy ground, an allotment, and an old sword he won when he was a lad not much older than me. The boggy shed was where we lived and the allotment was where most of our food came from. Sometimes he sent me to the nearby river to catch fish. I wasn't too good at that, so fish was off the menu more often than on it. Because he missed castle life, Sir Bozo spent the last of his loot on wooden battlements forthe shed and a drawbridge for the moat we didn't have. He tried to get a moat going by peeing from the battlements, and told me to do likewise. The flies were quite thick some days round Castle-de-Beurk-on-the-Allotment.

There wasn't a whole lot to do once I'd performed my menial duties, so it was just as well that I had a hobby. I carved things out of wood. Things like back-scratchers, animals, spoons, stuff like that. The day the big something happened that was to change my life I was sitting on the drawbridge (a plank) over the piddling moat putting the finishing touches to an egg.

'You have quite a gift for that,' a smooth voice said.

I looked up. Spiv Merlin. I'd only seen him once before, but I'd know him anywhere because he wasn't like anyone else. He was very tall, with ultra-black hair (obviously dyed) and a long droopy moustache, kind of oily-looking, that he was always stroking. There was a sweet smell about him, like overripe apples.

'Yours for a small fee,' I replied. 'Or a large one if you're feeling generous.'

He smirked. 'What would I do with a wooden egg? Eat it with wooden teeth?'

'It's an ornament. It's to go in the wooden eggcup I'm making next.'

'Really. Well, one thing I don't need is cheap ornaments.'

'Ornaments are only cheap if you don't pay much for them,' I said.

'They're even cheaper if you don't pay anything,' he chuckled, and quit the scene in a hurry. He'd noticed Sir Bozo heading our way.

'What was that arse-rag doing here?' Sir B wanted to know when he joined me.

'Wasting my time,' I said, polishing my egg with a cloth.

'Sire,' he said.

'Eh?' said I.

'You're supposed to call me sire because I'm your lord and master. I don't know how many times I've told you that.'

'Me neither. Lost count after time twenty-three.'

'Have you pulled the cabbages for lunch?'

'No.'

'Sire.'

'You're welcome.'

'Why haven't you pulled the cabbages like I told you to?'

'Because they're full of slugs.'

'Slugs? There are slugs in the cabbages?'

'Yes.'

'There are slugs in the cabbages and you left them there?'

'Yes.'

'Why?'

'They looked so happy.'

'You useless little peasant!' he cried, swiping me round the head. 'I can't remember the last time I had roast slug!'

And he rushed to the cabbage patch and started tearing up cabbages by the fistful. I rubbed my head and sighed. It was going to be roast slug six meals in a row. Just as I was getting used to being a vegetarian.

CHAPTER TWO

I don't usually dance in the same circles as bigwigs like Spivvel Merlin, so I was surprised when he approached me again the next day. Like before, I was sitting on the drawbridge, but this time I was oiling Sir Bozo's manky armour for the tournament he was jousting in tomorrow and the day after.

'Is he about?' Merlin asked.

'If you mean Sir B, no.'

'Good. Got a spot of business for you.'

I squinted up at him. 'Business? For me?'

'Yes. I want you to carve me a pair of wooden balls.'

You might not be surprised to hear that a minute's silence followed this.

'Well?' he said at last.

'Well what?'

'Have you nothing to say?'

'I've got lots to say, but they're all jokes you might not like.'

He dipped into a leather bag and took out two brightly coloured balls. Different colours on each one, swirly sort of pattern.

'Can you copy these?'

I examined the balls in his hand. 'Tricky,' I said.

'Why? You had no trouble carving that egg yesterday.'

'That was an egg. How perfect do you want the copies?'

'I want them exactly like these – I mean *exactly* – and in a hurry.'

'Sorry then, no can do. Perfection takes time.'

'You have till just after lunch tomorrow.'

'I'd need longer.'

'You can't have longer. I have to give these to my cl—' He stopped. Started half of that again. '...to my sister tomorrow afternoon. They were our father's, you see. He left them to her in his will.'

'Your father left his balls to your sister?'

'When he died.'

'Best time,' I said.

'I'd pay you.'

My eyes probably flared at this. The only money they usually saw was other people's. Sir Bozo paid me nothing. All I got from him in return for my services was a heap of straw to sleep on, and he said I should be grateful for that. Maybe I should've. He didn't have to give me straw.

'How much?' I asked Merlin.

He stroked his long black moustache. 'I'll give you half a groat. For the pair.'

I shook my bonce. 'Half a groat per ball or no deal.'

He snarled. Like most rich people he didn't like parting with money. 'Very well. But the paintwork better be good.'

'You want them painted too?'

'Of course I want them painted. If they're not they won't look like these, will they? You can paint, can't you?'

'Sure I can. I paint rats sometimes.'

'Rats?'

'Carved ones. I like to do them in bright colours.'

'You're a pretty weird kid, aren't you?' he said.

'You're a pretty weird legal wizard,' I answered.

'Less of the lip, boy. Can you paint my balls or not?'

'I suppose. Long as Sir Bozo doesn't suddenly find extra jobs for me.'

'Where is old Bozo anyway?' he asked.

'He's helping put the tourney tents up in return for pigeon soup and lumpy bread.'

Merlin laughed. 'The great Sir Bozo de Beurk putting up tents! How the mighty are fallen.'

'He's better off than me,' I said. 'He gets soup and bread, I get the burnt remains of last night's slug fritters.'

'So it's agreed then,' Merlin said.

'What is?'

'That you'll have a pair of balls exactly like these ready for me to collect by just after lunch tomorrow.'

'I'll give it a go.'

'Painted and dry,' he added.

'They will be.'

'If they're not perfect I won't pay you.'

'They'll be perfect.' I really wanted that groat.

Merlin handed me his balls. 'Guard them with your life and show them to no one. I'll be back just before two o'clock tomorrow.'

And he went.

I found a small block of wood and put the painted balls on the ground between my legs to copy them (balls, not legs). I'd just started work when I saw Sir

Bozo coming back. I closed my legs so he wouldn't see my balls and oiled some more of his armour. He wasn't in a great mood, but that was nothing new. Ever since his wife got the castle and almost everything else, he'd been going on and on – daily and knightly – about how hard-done-by he was.

'Here am I,' he muttered as he stepped onto the plank (I mean drawbridge), 'a knight who's fought battle after battle, rescued damsel after damsel—'

'One damsel,' I said. 'From a hedge. She was drunk.'

'—and I'm putting up tents for soup and bread, like some nobody.'

'Yeah, Spiv Merlin thought that was pretty funny too.'

I said this to myself, but he heard. His wits might not be too sharp, but he has the ears of a bat (they stick out).

'Merlin?' he said. 'He's been here again?'

'He wandered by.' I'd already said it, so I couldn't deny it.

'He wandered by and you told him I was putting up tents?'

'Yes, well, you know how these things slip out.'

He slapped me round the head.

'Stupid boy! Have you no loyalty?'

'I might have if you didn't do that every time I did something you didn't like.'

'That man,' he growled. 'Have you heard what he's done now?'

'Not yet,' I said, stroking my head. 'But I bet every last carrot on the allotment that I'm about to.'

'I'll tell you what he's done. He sued this wandering magician for not performing real magic like it said on the poster.'

'The carrots are mine!' I cried.

'The magician's been banished from the county, but before he went he was ordered to hand over all his props, so now he's just another strolling peasant, as if there weren't enough of those already. I hate that man!'

'The magician?'

'*Merlin*, you ragged urchin!'

And he stormed off, but not before landing another head smack. As he went I grabbed Merlin's balls and banged them together, wishing Bozo's head was between them. 'Ragged urchin yourself,' I said, turning away to spit. But then I heard a shout and looked back. Right where Sir Bozo had been stood a boy of about my age, in clothes even dirtier and more wrinkled than mine. The shout hadn't come from him, though, but from a pasty-faced weasel-eyed man on a dusty carthorse who'd yelled at him for not jumping out of the way as he clopped up. It was nothing to do with me and I should have just minded my own business, but I was still annoyed at being so badly treated by Sir B, so I took the little block of wood I'd started work on and tossed it under the carthorse's hooves. This caused the horse to stumble and its rider to fly over its neck and land neatly (face down) on the drawbridge I was sitting on.

'Hey, good bird impression,' I said to the man suddenly at my feet.

He hadn't seen me toss the wood, but I wasn't surprised when he jumped up and slapped me round the head.

'Cheeky young bleeder,' he snarled.

Then he got back in the saddle, whipped the horse's flanks like it was all its fault, and rode on.

Three head slaps in two minutes. It's no fun being a peasant kid in this day and age. No fun at all...